D0378808

Purchased from
Multnomah County Library
Title Wave Used Bookstore
216 NE Knott St, Portland, OR
503-988-5021

CHILL FACTOR

CHILL FACTOR

Peter Turnbull

This first world edition published in Great Britain 2005 by
SEVERN HOUSE PUBLISHERS LTD of
9–15 High Street, Sutton, Surrey SM1 1DF.
This first world edition published in the USA 2005 by
SEVERN HOUSE PUBLISHERS INC of
595 Madison Avenue, New York, N.Y. 10022.

Copyright © 2005 by Peter Turnbull.

All rights reserved.
The moral right of the author has been asserted.

British Library Cataloguing in Publication Data

Turnbull, Peter, 1950–
    Chill factor
    1. Hennessey, George (Fictitious character) - Fiction
    2. Yellich, Somerled (Fictitious character) - Fiction
    3. Police - England - Yorkshire - Fiction
    4. Murder - Investigation - England - Yorkshire - Fiction
    5. Detective and mystery stories
    I. Title
    823.9'14 [F]

ISBN-10 : 0-7278-6275-8 (cased)
            0-7278- 9147-2 (paper)

Except where actual historical events and characters are being
described for the storyline of this novel, all situations in this
publication are fictitious and any resemblance to living persons
is purely coincidental.

Typeset by Palimpsest Book Production Ltd.,
Polmont, Stirlingshire, Scotland.
Printed and bound in Great Britain by
MPG Books Ltd., Bodmin, Cornwall.

One

in which a murder is confirmed.

It was upon seeing the body for the second time that the man realized that he was looking at a corpse. It had been a warm dawn that day, which had grown into a hot forenoon and then into an even hotter afternoon. Seeing a man, a young man in jeans and T-shirt, lying on the expanse of grass was not, he'd thought, at all unusual. It was midweek when most employed persons are at work, but only most, for those that work 'unsocial hours' are compensated by having free time at unusual times of the week. Further, sadly in York and its surroundings, unemployment is not at all unknown and for a man with little money and much time there is often nothing else to do, reasoned the man, but lie on the green stuff under the yellow thing, especially on a day like that day; hot and very sultry. The man had walked on, leaving the other man to his peace on the grass. He found the heat of the sun uncomfortable and had been anxious to reach the shade offered by the buildings at Micklegate. He had hurried along the wall and left it at Micklegate Bar. He had completed his business in the city, visiting his dentist, by appointment, and had taken the opportunity to do a little shopping: a Panama hat for himself, a small token for his wife – something to let her

1

know how much he appreciated her, and that he thought of her both often and warmly. He had subsequently rejoined the wall again at Micklegate Bar to walk the section to Baile Hill and hence to his modest terraced house on Clementhorpe Street. As the man drew level with Lower Priory Street to his left and below him, he once again saw the same man lying where he had been lying when he had passed nearly two hours earlier. What made the second sight of the man unusual was that the man had not apparently moved. He was still, so far as the walker on the wall could see, in precisely the same position as he had been when he was first noticed. It was then that the man realized that he was looking at a corpse. Other wall-walkers would doubtless have seen the man and also assumed that he was sleeping, and the people who walked along Lower Priory Road may not have seen him at all, that section of grass being elevated above eye level from the street. It is an area of grass on to which children climb to throw frisbees to each other or other people clamber on to to exercise their dogs. The man plunged his hand into his trouser pocket, extracting his mobile phone. He pressed three nines and asked for the police. When he was connected he further asked for the police to attend at that location and explained why in a voice which he tried hard to make sound calm and collected.

The white police patrol car arrived within a matter of minutes, as indeed the man expected it to do, this being the very heart of the ancient city. It drove purposefully down Fairfax Street, between the rows of nineteenth-century terraced houses, but without the blue light lapping or the klaxons sounding; there being no need for either. As the car approached, the man moved his arm and the police driver flashed the car's headlights, once, as a response. The constable halted the car at the bottom of Fairfax Street and got out. The man pointed to the body lying on the grass beneath him. The constable crossed

Lower Priory Street, levered himself up on to the grassed terrace which ran between the street and the wall, and walked cautiously towards the supine man. He looked down at the man, then up at the man on the wall and nodded. 'You were correct to phone us, sir.' He raised his voice so as to allow it to carry up to the battlements, twenty feet distant and fifteen feet above him.

'Is he dead?' the man called back.

'Not for me to say, sir. Can you come down here? We'll have to take a statement.'

'Certainly . . . ' the man looked left and then right, 'back to Micklegate Bar steps would be quicker, take me about ten minutes.' He turned and, as he did so, saw the constable reach for the radio which was attached to his shirt collar and begin to speak into it.

The scene looked very familiar. First there were the police vehicles, with one having turned on its flashing blue light so as to invite a degree of urgency into the activity. There was the blue and white police tape strung along the length of the elevated grass terrace; there were folk on the wall standing and watching the events unfold below them, an annoying, for the police, aspect of human behaviour which they cannot control or prevent and which has been dubbed 'the ogle factor'. Finally, standing with the constables on the terrace was the turban-headed police surgeon who carried himself, as did the officers, with calm and poise. It was then that Hennessey knew the 'apparent' code 41 wasn't going to be 'apparent' but was going to be 'actual'.

He parked his car behind the black, windowless mortuary van and walked to the terrace, climbed the steps on to the grass, ducked under the police tape, and approached Dr Mann, DS Yellich and a uniformed officer.

'Hardly worth the drive, sir.' Yellich welcomed him with a smile.

'I was on my way back from Northallerton, your call was diverted to my car phone,' Hennessey replied dryly, a little offended that Yellich could even think for one moment that he would drive the two hundred yards from Micklegate Bar Police Station to Lower Priory Street. 'So what have we got?'

'Adult of the male sex, sir.' Yellich knelt and peeled back the plastic sheeting which covered the corpse, revealing the head of a young man, with a 'hard' face, so thought Hennessey. 'Dr Mann here has pronounced his life extinct.'

'He was shot,' Dr Mann offered.

'Shot!' Hennessey turned to the police surgeon. 'That's unusual.'

'Even more unusual is the manner of the shooting, sir. It's not as though he was blasted with a shotgun, which is not unknown in the Vale . . . one irate farmer blasts another . . . this fella was shot with a small-calibre gun, very close up, to the head, just below the left ear. There is no exit wound, the bullet must have whizzed round and round the brain before running out of momentum. It is what I understand as a "professional hit" . . . well, it appears to be that.'

'Better,' Hennessey grunted, 'too early to say what it is but I know what you mean.' He ran a liver-spotted hand through his silver hair. 'When was he found, and by whom?'

'Member of the public, sir.' Yellich consulted his notebook. 'One Ernest Reeve . . . middle-aged gentleman – lives very near here. He was walking the wall back from the centre of York. He had noticed the deceased as he'd walked in. When he walked back, saw that he hadn't moved . . . initially he thought he was resting in the sun . . . called three nines, the attending constable confirmed the man appeared to be deceased and in suspicious circumstance . . . and we are here.'

Hennessey checked his watch. 'Coming up to three p.m.

He must have been left here in the night and nobody noticed anything of concern until less than an hour ago?'

Yellich shrugged. 'Apparently not, sir. The terrace is elevated and can't be seen from the street. Anyone walking the walls or looking out from the upper rooms of the houses there must have assumed he was resting. The injury can only be seen if you are as close as we are.'

'Aye . . . well, that's of little interest. What is of interest is who is he and who, if any, saw what or heard what, if anything? Has the pathologist been summoned?'

'Yes, sir. She's on her way.'

'Right. If you could organize a house-to-house, please, Sergeant. All the houses on the street and the roads that would be likely used to access and leave.'

'Very good, sir.' Yellich left the group, calling to a uniformed sergeant.

'You have no further need of me, Mr Hennessey,' Dr Mann said softly. 'I'll take my leave. I have another scene to attend, an elderly lady out in Murton. Heatstroke, I would anticipate. In this heat we are going to lose many of our elderly.'

'Yes, thank you, doctor.'

'Fourteen forty-five hours.'

'Sorry?'

'I confirmed life extinct at fourteen forty-five this day.'

'Ah . . . yes'

'Sergeant Yellich has the time but the pathologist will probably want to know the time of confirmation of L.E. when she arrives.'

'Yes, thank you.'

Dr Mann walked slowly, calmly away from the scene of crime. Hennessey turned to the constable. He thought he looked ashen-faced. 'Is this your first corpse?'

'No, sir, road-traffic-accident victim was, this is my second.'

'I see. Well, it won't be your last.'

'That's what Sergeant Youngman said.' The constable forced a grin.

'Do you know if the scenes of crime people have attended?'

'Photographs have been taken, sir.'

'Good . . . good.' Hennessey spoke absentmindedly as he glanced up the length of Fairfax Street just as a red and white Riley RMA turned into the street.

'Oh . . .' the constable gasped, 'lovely old car.'

'You haven't seen it before?'

'No, sir'

'It's Dr D'Acre – our forensic pathologist. The car was first registered in 1947 . . . still in daily use.'

'Really, sir?'

'Well, as you see, the doctor dotes on it.'

'So would I if it were mine, sir. What a lovely old lady of a vehicle.'

'You'll see it each time you attend a suspicious death in this division. It's a bit infamous in that respect, every time somebody is murdered the old red and white Riley appears.'

'Still a lovely vehicle, sir.'

'Absolutely, wasn't suggesting otherwise. The doctor told me once she has an arrangement with a garage proprietor: he services it for her and is able to obtain the difficult-to-find spare parts and has extracted a promise from her that if she ever wishes to sell it he is to be offered first refusal. She will never sell it, it was her father's first and only car, and she intends to bequeath it to her son in the fullness of time, and in fairness she has told the garage proprietor that, but he lives in hope and gives his all to the car in the chance it may one day be his.' Hennessey saw no reason why the constable should not know of Dr D'Acre and her car; she made no secret of it and by telling the young constable, Hennessey hoped he had fostered a sense of belonging in him, of being part of the team. Dr D'Acre, slender, short hair, lithe yet clearly strong of limb, got out of her car, having parked it behind Hennessey's car, and walked, wearing a serious, single-minded expression, so observed Hennessey, to where he and the constable waited.

'Deceased male,' Hennessey said after courtesies and pleasantries had been exchanged, as the constable knelt to peel back the plastic sheet that had lain over the body.

'So I see.' Dr D'Acre glanced up at the wall above and saw with some relief that two constables were 'moving on' the curious populace. 'Wouldn't want to take a rectal temperature reading in front of an audience,' she commented. 'You haven't erected a tent?'

'The indication is that the body has been dumped, ma'am. Unless you find any reason not to, we plan to remove the body as speedily as possible. Had it been a buried corpse that had become unearthed, then, yes, a tent would have been inflated.'

'I see.' Dr D'Acre knelt. 'Well, of immediate note is what appears to be a bullet entry wound behind the left ear.' She spoke for her own benefit into a handheld battery-operated cassette tape recorder. She peeled the black plastic sheet back and surveyed the body. 'The deceased is fully clothed, has no other evident injuries, he is clean and appears well nourished.' She switched off the tape recorder and looked up at DCI Hennessey. 'Someone will have noticed him missing if not already so, then soon . . . no down-and-out he.'

'Always useful,' Hennessey replied, again sweeping his hand through his hair, 'an early ID of the corpse that is. Nothing in his pockets, though . . .' DS Yellich reported that he'd checked as soon as Dr Mann had pronounced life extinct. 'As if someone wanted to hinder our progress.'

'Or he had been searched for something. But that's your area of expertise, your department, not mine.'

'Point,' Hennessey mumbled. 'It's worth bearing that in mind.'

'Could you help me turn him over, please?' Dr D'Acre appealed to the constable. 'I'll take a rectal temperature reading before the crowd gathers again. Then if you have no further need, no more photographs to be taken, he can be transported to the York District. I'll perform the PM as soon as he arrives. Will you be representing the police, Chief Inspector?'

'Yes ma'am. DS Yellich has things well covered here, so yes, I'll be there.'

'Heard but not seen, it seems, sir.' The uniformed sergeant stood square on to Yellich but was nevertheless deferential in his attitude. 'A few folks report a car in the night, arrived slowly, came down Victor Street, turned into Lower Priory Street, here, nothing unusual in that, but what made folk notice was that it sped away up Hampden Street . . . real tyre-squealing number, by all accounts.'

'Time?' asked Yellich calmly.

'About five a.m., just as it was getting light.'

'Not many cars about then.' Yellich smiled.

'CCTV footage you mean, sir?'

Yellich nodded. 'Indeed I do. I'll get on to that right away. Can you please carry on with the house-to-house? Someone might have seen something.'

'Very good, sir.'

It was, thought Hennessey, the same scene played over and over again, not quite like watching a video loop or listening to a vinyl record that is stuck in a groove because the central character was always different and no two scripts were ever the same. Each scene was different, yet each had a very familiar quality. What was the same was the setting, the pathology laboratory at York City Hospital. What was also the same were the living characters, Eric Filey, the mortuary assistant, Dr Louise D'Acre, and finally, one observing for the police, being in this case George Hennessey. The fourth person, the deceased, lay face up on a stainless-steel table, one of four in the laboratory, with a starched white towel draped over his genitals. Dr D'Acre adjusted the microphone which was attached to a stainless-steel anglepoise arm and which was bolted to the ceiling above the table.

'Please give this case a file number, Jenny,' Dr D'Acre spoke into the microphone, 'we have no name as yet.' She glanced over to where Hennessey stood against the wall, keeping a respectful distance from the dissecting table and wearing green overalls with his feet encased in disposable slippers. He shook his head in confirmation that the deceased was still unidentified. 'The deceased is a well-nourished man in his late twenties or early thirties, and of European appearance. He has no distinguishing features, no tattoos, for example, which might aid identification. There is extensive bruising around the torso but that would not in itself have been fatal. He appears to be clean, no dirt under the fingernails for example. He was a man who gave attention to his personal hygiene.' She flexed the man's legs. 'Rigor is beginning to establish. Death occurred within the last twelve hours.' She glanced at Hennessey. 'We have had this conversation before, you and I.'

'Indeed.' Hennessey smiled and nodded. 'Life imitating art, you determine the how but not the when.'

'That's it, Chief Inspector. All I am prepared to say is within twelve hours of the present, possibly within eighteen hours.' She returned her attention to the corpse. 'Let's have a look in his mouth before it seizes shut. The mouth is a veritable goldmine of information.' She opened the mouth, forcing the jaw, Hennessey noted, with some effort. Rigor was definitely establishing itself. 'Ah . . . just got it open in time. Yes, again, evidence of him looking after himself: recent dentistry and British dentistry too . . . not a foreigner . . . and so dental records will be able to confirm his identity if all else fails. Dentists in the UK are obliged to keep their records for eleven years; this gentleman visited his dentist well within that time, probably within the last twelve months. Kept clean teeth too: no food residue at all is noted. Good man, brushed twice daily. Now, the cause of death, well . . . immediately obvious in the gunshot wound to the skull, behind the left ear, there is powder residue around the entry wound which indicates the gun was only a matter of inches from the skull when it was fired.'

'Murder?'

'Oh yes, this is no firearms accident, this is murder most foul. As I noted at the scene, there is no exit wound and so the bullet will still be in there somewhere. It's not going anywhere, so I'll return to it in due course. Looking at his limbs, his feet and his forearms show signs of burning. Mr Filey, can we have a photograph, please? Would you care to take a look at this, Chief Inspector?' Hennessey too approached the table as Eric Filey reached for a 35mm single lens camera with a flash attachment. 'You see these linear burn marks, on his forearms and part above his ankles?'

'Yes. What causes such?'

'Electricity. You see how his body hair is absent?'

'Yes . . . yes, so it is quite smooth skin about the burns.' He stepped aside to allow Eric Filey to take close-up photographs of the injuries.

'Wire was attached to his body and held in place with tape. When the tape was removed it pulled out the body hair that it had covered. He was tortured before he was murdered.'

'Looks like Dr Mann was correct.'

'What did he say?' Dr D'Acre also stepped away from the table to allow Eric Filey access to the corpse. 'That it was a "professional hit". Tortured, then executed. This is gangland . . . going to be a tough nut to crack.' 'I'm sure you will give it your best shot.' She eyed him warmly but refrained from smiling. 'No pun intended.' 'I'd like to think we will, but I've been here before . . . murders committed by organized crime, these boys know how to cover their tracks . . . sometimes there isn't even a body.' He turned and walked back to the wall. 'We just find out that someone known to be associated with organized crime has disappeared . . . They'll be at the bottom of the Ouse.'

'Often that's worse, not knowing. At least this young gentleman's family will have a body to bury and a grave to visit. Well, let's see what he had for his last meal. You may care to take a deep breath.' Dr D'Acre placed a scalpel over the stomach, inserted into the flesh and drew it downwards towards the groin, turning her head away as escaping stomach gasses hissed. 'Oh, smelled worse,' she said, 'but it's never pleasant.'

Hennessey didn't comment, but he too had smelled worse. He breathed shallowly until the smell of the stomach gas had been subsumed by the overriding smell of the formaldehyde of the pathology laboratory.

Dr D' Acre peered into the stomach. 'And that,' she said, 'is why we have both smelled worse. His stomach is empty. Something has to corrupt to form gas, either food in the stomach has to corrupt or the body in the first stage of decomposition corrupts, but here, the man was alive but without food and for any stomach to be as devoid of food as this stomach is devoid of food, then he couldn't have eaten for three or four days . . . yet he looks strong and well nourished.'

'He was starved?' Hennessey offered.

'It would certainly seem so. Food was deliberately with-held from him. The bullet was quick and painless but prior to that . . . it was prolonged and painful. Ever been hungry? I mean really hungry?'

'No, lucky I.' Hennessey shuddered at the thought of the alternative. 'Fifty plus summers upon this planet and never been hungry once.'

'Forty-three for me. Being born at the right time and the right place is something we shouldn't take for granted. How about you, Eric, ever known hunger?'

'Not once, Dr D'Acre.' Eric Filey, rotund with a jovial manner, so had found Hennessey whenever he had attended a post-mortem at York District Hospital. 'Thirty-seven summers for me . . . Longest without food? Twenty-four hours once when I was a teenager, but I hadn't got this weight then and it was summer, this sort of weather, so I didn't need food as much as I would have done in the winter months.'

'We count ourselves as indeed fortunate.' Dr D'Acre looked at the corpse. 'We should, I think, take a closer look at the wound before we remove the brain. You have photographed the wound as it is, Eric?'

'Yes, ma'am.'

'Good. Then I'll remove the skin.' Dr D'Acre took a scalpel and made an incision round the circumference of the head and then peeled the flesh away from the wound. 'Another photograph now, please, Eric . . . of this . . .'

'Yes, ma'am.' Eric Filey advanced on the dissecting table, camera in hand, and took three photographs of the wound to the skull, as seen once the flesh had been removed.

Dr D'Acre nodded her thanks to him and then returned her attention to the corpse. 'So . . . we'll now have a look inside his skull, see what damage the bullet did. Can I have the circular saw, please, Eric?'

Filey handed Dr D'Acre a power-operated saw with a

circular blade. She switched the machine on, causing the blade to revolve at high speed, making a high-pitched sound as it did so. She put it to the side of the skull of the deceased just above the right ear and Hennessey grimaced at the sound of the blade against the bone. Within a matter of minutes and with evident skill, Dr D'Acre had sawn completely round the skull, severing it laterally. She lifted the top of the skull off and revealed the brain. 'Quite a lot of damage is noticeable,' she said clearly for the benefit of the microphone. 'I'll extract the brain completely.' She took a scalpel and severed the brain from the spinal column at the cerebral cortex and lifted it from the skull and placed it on a stainless-steel tray. She examined it closely. 'And here,' she said, 'is the bullet. It has whizzed round and round the brain before being stopped when it came into contact with the skull. By then it had clearly run out of momentum so that it could neither burst out of the skull not back into the brain. A pair of tweezers please, Eric.'

Filey handed her a pair of tweezers.

'Makes my job easier.' Dr D'Acre carefully extracted the bullet from the brain tissue, having gripped it with the tweezers. 'Saves me from slicing the brain until I found it. Dare say I could have X-rayed the brain to locate it, but that's time consuming, slicing a little off at a time is more efficient.' She dropped the bullet on to a second tray. 'Do you have a production bag, Chief Inspector?'

'With my clothing in the changing room. I'll go and collect it.' Hennessey padded awkwardly out of the pathology laboratory, the paper-based disposable overalls rustling as he walked. He returned a few moments later with a small self-sealing cellophane sachet, which he opened and extended in Dr D'Acre's direction. Using the tweezers, Dr D'Acre picked up the bullet and placed it in the sachet. He smiled his thanks and returned to his place by the wall.

'That,' Dr D'Acre tapped the side of the shiny steel table, '– that concludes this particular post-mortem. Death was due to a single gunshot wound to the head but prior to death he was deprived of food for three or four days and was tortured with electricity.'

'I'd like to arrange our scenes of crime officers to come and lift his fingerprints if that could be arranged?'

'Of course. They can liaise directly with the mortuary officials for that. Why? Do you think he's known to you?'

George Hennessey scratched an itch on the back of his hand. 'Well . . . "ex-con" comes to the forefront of my mind. Sergeant Yellich commented that he had a "hard" expression even in death. Well-nourished and clean, that says prison life, and his death, that is gangland-execution style. The underworld is close-knit, you don't get accepted unless you've completed a rite of passage as a guest of Her Majesty, so yes, in my waters I think we'll know this gentleman.'

'Still, he's too young to be here.' Dr D'Acre glanced at the corpse under the glare of the filament bulbs, shielded by Perspex covers. 'He's not the youngest murder victim I have dissected and any murder victim, by the fact that they have been murdered, is not ready to be here but I always feel for those under thirty years as he seems to be. What life could have been his he and we will never know.' She paused. 'Well, I'll have my report faxed to you as soon as it's typed, probably be tomorrow morning.' Dr D'Acre glanced up at the clock on the wall of the laboratory. 'I won't finish it before five now and the secretaries knock off then – all got boyfriends to rush home for: eat, change, then out with their fellas. They'll pick it up, first thing. It'll be with you before lunch tomorrow.'

'I'll arrange for SOCO to come over and lift his prints. We should have a result on those by tomorrow lunchtime if he's known and I feel sure he will be.'

It was 16.40 hours.

Chill Factor

George Hennessey read the file on Gary 'Hammer' Sledge. He looked over the top of the file, caught eye contact with Yellich and said, 'He's been a busy boy.'

'Really, skipper?' Yellich sipped his tea.

'Well you'll see for yourself in a moment but he came to our notice when he was fourteen, got an official warning, but it was enough to put him on the system. Then he was before the juvenile bench for shoplifting, theft of cars and theft from cars and assault, all whilst still a minor. Eventually they got fed up with him and deemed him in need of "care and control" and sent him down for six months. He bounced in and out of gaol over the next ten years more, mostly for crimes of violence . . . most was five years for armed robbery . . . quite lenient. He probably was a minor player in whatever it was that went down . . . last released just two weeks ago.'

'Two weeks at liberty and he gets a bullet in the head.'

'Yes.' Hennessey reached for his mug of tea and sipped it, savouring the taste. 'Probably less than two weeks liberty if Dr D'Acre is correct about being starved for three of four days prior to being iced, that implies he was held against his will for that length of time. So out for just over a week then abducted by more than one person. It would take a gang to overpower him.' He paused. 'His numbers make him twenty-nine, just a few days short of his thirtieth.'

'Some present.'

'Yes, I can think of better ways to celebrate a birthday.' Hennessey glanced out of the small window of his office to the walls, at that moment thronged with tourists, clearly tourists, looking this way and that, laden down with cameras, moving in groups or in pairs, dressed in 'loud', colourful clothing. 'His next of kin is given as his parents, they live on the Tang Hall estate.'

15

'Part of York that those out there are unlikely to see,' Yellich said, following Hennessey's gaze, 'or even would want to see.'

'Indeed.' Hennessey stood. 'Let's go and break some bad news . . . never easy, just various degrees of difficulty.'

Mr and Mrs Sledge lived in a ground-floor, three-bedroomed flat in a low-rise block on Fourth Avenue, Tang Hall. Yellich halted the car outside the drab-looking brick-built building and he and Hennessey got out.

'Could be worse,' Yellich observed. 'I mean at least they get to look out across the allotments; better than looking across this narrow street at somebody else's lace curtains.'

Hennessey looked around him. Tang Hall had never been his favourite part of York: he found it oppressive, knew it to be 'rough' and given to violence among its residents. Motorbikes stood chained against concrete lamp-posts, curtains twitched as tenants became aware of the police presence. Hennessey knew that neither he nor Yellich needed uniforms to be identified as 'busies' in Tang Hall.

They walked up the narrow path between low privet hedges with lawn beyond, which were kept in good order by the local authority, pushed open the door at the entrance to the block of flats and knocked on the ground-floor door to the right as they entered.

The door was opened aggressively by a strong-looking, silver-haired man dressed in vest and summer slacks. He was barefoot. 'He's not here,' he snarled. 'Our Gary, he's not here.' He made to shut the door but Hennessey held it open.

'We know.' Hennessey spoke calmly.

'Why? You arrested him again? He's only been out of Long Sutton for two weeks.'

'No.' Hennessey maintained a calm voice. 'No, we haven't arrested him. I'm afraid we've got some bad news for you. May we come in? I'm DCI Hennessey, this is DS Yellich.'

Colour drained from the man's face, his jaw sagged. 'Muriel,' he called, 'Muriel.' Then he stepped aside and Hennessey and Yellich entered the small hallway. 'Go through,' the man invited. His voice was now frail-sounding. At the end of the hall was the kitchen, in the doorway a late middle-aged woman – clearly 'Muriel', assumed Hennessey – stood wringing a tea towel in her hands. Colour, similarly, had drained from her face.

The living room at the Sledge household was untidy with tabloid newsprint strewn about and the fire grate, as in many houses that summer, had become a receptacle for anything combustible. It did, however, seem clean, and both officers accepted the invitation to sit down. Mrs Sledge also sat as Mr Sledge stood, manfully, in front of the fireplace.

'Well . . . I'm afraid we have to tell you that Gary is deceased.' There was no easy way to say it and so Hennessey just said it, though he hoped his voice tone was soft and gentle.

Mrs Sledge started to whimper and then ran from the room and into another room – Hennessey presumed it would be the bedroom. Mr Sledge looked stunned. 'I knew it was trouble as soon as you pulled up outside. I had my last brush with the law twenty years back, but I can still recognize lawmen. You used to call to lift me, these last years you've been calling to lift our Gary or our Shane, sometimes you'd lift them both together, so I knew it was trouble . . . Never thought it was this type of trouble. Mr Hennessey, did you say?'

'Yes, Hennessey.'

'Like the brandy.' Mr Sledge forced a smile.

'Similar . . . my name has an "e" before the "y."'

'Hennessey, easy name to remember. And your name, sir . . . that sounds unusual.'

'Yellich . . . yes, of uncertain origin . . . probably an Eastern European name that became corrupted at some point, making it sound more accessible to British ears.' The aside, he believed, would ease the tension.

'Oh . . .' The man seemed to both officers to be in a state of shock, understandably so, they felt, and they were quite happy to let him ramble. He collected himself and asked, 'So what? I mean how . . . ?'

'He was shot.'

'Shot!'

'I'm afraid so, Mr Sledge.'

'Oh, not the man on the news? Last night the local news had a story about a man found by the walls who'd been shot . . . That wasn't our Gary?'

'I'm afraid it was . . . The fingerprints were taken. Gary having a record, and a local record, the match was made this morning. We came straight out here. I am very sorry.'

'There's no mistake?'

'None . . . The fingerprints are an unmistakeable match.'

'But who'd . . . ?'

'Which is the question we would hope you could help answer. Do you know of anyone who would want to harm Gary?'

'Not offhand . . . He was a con, he liked a fight. People like me and my two lads, we make friends, we also make enemies . . . more enemies than friends. For every one who'd stand next to you in a fight, there's three that would put the boot in when you're down.'

'Did he live here?'

'No, he had a tenancy of his own on the estate just round the corner on Sixth Avenue. I have the keys to it . . . You'll be wanting them.' He turned and took a set of keys from a jar which stood on the mantelpiece. He handed them to Hennessey. 'Our Shane would be the one to ask about friends and enemies.'

'Where would we find Shane?'

'Armley.'

'Armley? The prison?'

'Yes, he's doing a three stretch for receiving stolen goods. The idiot only tried to sell them to an undercover busy. Our Shane just hasn't got what our Gary had. Our Gary was going somewhere. Can we see his body? I don't think our Muriel will believe he's dead otherwise.'

'Of course, that's easy to arrange.' Hennessey thought, but didn't add, that it would also serve to confirm his identity, though he doubted that such confirmation would be required. Instead he asked when Mr Sledge had last seen his son.

'Few days ago, Sunday. Both boys have got single-person tenancies on the estate, but we don't visit daily – they're adults and are making their own way in the world – but when they're on the outside, one or both, depending, they call round here at eleven o'clock Sunday morning. The two, or three, of us go for a few pots, get back around three in the afternoon. Muriel will have made us a roast meal, we eat it, they go home, see them again the next Sunday. Each family has its routines . . . That's ours.'

'Thank you.' Hennessey stood. Yellich followed his lead.

'We'll go and visit your son's address, might be something there for us.'

'You'll let us know about viewing his body?'

'You can talk directly with the hospital about that, Mr Sledge.' Hennessey took out his card and handed it to Sledge. 'That's my name and phone number. If you have difficulty with accessing Gary's body, call me, I'll do what I can to help but you shouldn't have any problems.'

'Thank you. It's appreciated.'

Hennessey and Yellich drove the short distance from Fourth to Sixth Avenue. It was an easy distance to walk but without commenting, both men realized it would have been insensitive in the extreme to leave their vehicle parked outside the Sledges' house, and so they drove, Yellich not needing to take the car beyond the second gear.

Gary Sledge had lived in a low-rise block similar to his parents' tenancy except that in his case, his flat had been on the top floor, four flights of stairs from the ground level. Hennessey and Yellich stood in front of the door and listened for any sounds from within the flat. Not hearing anything, Hennessey knocked on the door with the classic police officer's knock, which he had first heard when about eight years of age, knock, knock . . . knock. There was no response. He tried the door. It was unlocked. He pushed it open. The interior of the flat was a scene of confusion, chaos and mayhem: drawers had been emptied of their contents, furniture turned over, carpets pulled up, bedding torn from the bed, clothes flung out of the wardrobe, even the small refrigerator had been ransacked.

'Starved, electrocuted, his flat turned over . . . somebody wanted something from Gary Sledge, better get SOCO here, this is a crime scene. Then we'll do a door-to-door . . . Somebody must have heard something.'

'Very good, boss.' Yellich plunged his hand into his jacket pocket and extracted his mobile phone, as he and Hennessey walked out of the flat to the landing and the seven other flats that shared the staircase.

Two

in which an elderly lady with remarkable powers of observation is met and Yellich makes a prison visit.

'Heard banging and crashing about, but nothing unusual.'

'That's not unusual?' Hennessey raised an eyebrow.

'Well, don't know where you live, sir, but this is Tang Hall, and above me is young Sledge.' The elderly man was smartly but casually dressed. His appearance said 'ex-serviceman': highly polished shoes, erect bearing, pencil-line moustache, defending the threshold of his flat, showing no fear of Hennessey, but at the same time exhibiting a clear deference. 'Sledge, well he's Gary Sledge, one of the Sledge family . . . top-dog family on the estate. If the Sledges have it in for you, you've got bad news but they leave me alone. I don't pose any threat, you see.'

'You don't?'

'No, widower, live alone, quiet life, stay in most of the time. Don't challenge their rule at "The Hall". Other families . . . family called Davidson, their sons came of age and started to flex their muscles on the estate, then it was showdown at the OK Corral time. Davidsons were hospitalized and their windows put through, that's the Sledges'

21

answer to anyone who threatens them. Me, I'm just an old guy, they leave me alone.'

'I see.'

'I also benefit from living on the same stair.'

'Benefit?'

'Well, in my experience, families . . . neighbours like the Sledges don't want to soil their own nest. They're more likely to pick fights with families who live in the next street than the same street.'

Hennessey didn't comment, but how wrong he thought the man was in that observation. He could think of a few next-door-neighbour feuds that had been long-lasting and had ended up in bloodshed and murder. 'So when did you hear the banging and crashing about?'

'Few days ago . . . over the weekend . . . Wasn't unusual because young Sledge often came home after a night in town and smashed up his flat. He had a lot of anger in him which came out after he'd had a few beers. The drink went in, the anger came out. Then he'd tidy up the place. I'd hear scraping of furniture. Sounds like that went on over a longer time than the smashing did and the banging . . . Your flat getting trashed takes ten minutes . . . then the sounds of it being put back together take an hour.'

'Fair enough.'

'But on this occasion there were a few things that were different . . . come to think of it they were a lot different.'

'For example?'

'Well . . .' The man looked down for a moment and then at Hennessey again. 'Well, the first thing is that the banging about took place during the day . . . Usually he rearranges his furniture at midnight or later but this was the middle of the afternoon. Started early that day, I thought, got himself a bottle and taken it into the park, came back feeling angry, took it out on his furniture and spent the rest of the day sleeping it off. So I thought. But the next day there wasn't the usual sounds of him trying to put things back again and there wasn't the usual wreckage outside in the street waiting for the bin men to collect.'

'Wreckage?'

'The bits of furniture that had been smashed beyond repair . . . coffee tables usually, the coffee table is always a victim, gets kicked into little pieces, and a few days later he's seen walking back to his flat carrying a new second-hand coffee table or small television – that's another favourite target . . . things like that, but this time there was no wreckage in the street neatly piled up next to the wheelie bins on collection day.'

'I see.'

'I did wonder if he was alright, that crossed my mind.'

'You didn't check on him?'

'I didn't want to get involved with the Sledges.' The elderly man shook his head. 'Sorry . . . a bit . . . a bit something . . . callous . . . but . . . if an elderly lady or gent was in that flat and I hadn't seen him or her for a few days I'd be up there, believe me I would.'

'I do believe you, sir.'

'But, the Sledges . . . have you met them?'

'Yes, just come from Mr and Mrs Sledge's . . .'

'Well, I've lived on the Hall for a good few years. I watched the Sledge boys grow up, watched them show a hard side almost from day one. They can be pleasant to visitors if they need to be. Never made a secret of their criminal activity, but they can show a civil side for a while . . . But they have another side to them. I mean, even if I was the one to raise the alarm that led to Gary's body being discovered, they'd turn on me for that. It's the way the family thinks. I can't be doing with that sort of grief at my time of life. I've been keeping so far away from that family that I wouldn't even dare do them a favour.'

'I see . . . that's interesting, very interesting indeed. Very helpful.'

'I'd like to think I was . . . Haven't told you much.'

'More than you think . . .' Hennessey smiled. 'I can tell you that you didn't hear Gary Sledge smashing his flat up, you heard someone else in there.'

'Really?'

'Yes, really, either smashing it up or searching for something. Probably the latter. And you've told me that whoever it was wasn't frightened of the Sledges.'

'Then that's somebody off the estate. No one on "The Hall" would dare do that to one of the Sledges.'

'That is my thinking. Thank you for your help.' Hennessey turned and walked back up the stairway to Gary Sledge's flat, ducked under the blue and white police tape and entered the corridor. A Scenes of Crime Officer in a white disposable overall nodded in recognition of him.

'It's not a scene of violence, sir, not in my opinion, based on my experience.'

'*This* is not violence?' Hennessey looked about him at the disarray, the confusion.

'No, sir, with respect, nothing has been damaged, there's no blood anywhere but many signs of gloved hands, two pairs. This is more in the manner of a very messy burglary.'

'Ah, I see what you mean, Mr . . . ?'

'Parr, sir . . . Thomas Parr.' He was a tall, slightly built man.

'Thank you. So, Mr Parr,' Hennessey thought Parr to be in his late thirties, old enough to be able to say 'in my experience' with some credibility, '– so no act of violence against the person took place here? No fight, no assault?'

'None, sir, and the door wasn't forced, yet it has three locks on it.'

'Three?' Hennessey turned. 'So it has. I hadn't noticed

the one at the bottom. Young Mr Sledge was clearly
fearful of being broken into.'

'Yes, sir, but it wasn't a burglary. We found quite a bit of
jewellery . . . some watches . . . we also found an empty cardboard box, a shoebox which was pushed well under the bed'

'As if it had contained something of value?'

'That's our thinking, sir. This is the scene of a search.
After the felons let themselves in using the door keys.'

'That's what myself and Sergeant Yellich thought but it's
useful to have your opinion, Mr Parr, and they either found
what they were searching for, or they didn't, but took what
was in the shoebox anyway, as if it was his hard cash store.'

'That's our reading of this scene, sir.'

'And there were two of them?'

'Yes, sir, one was wearing gloves which left a smooth
impression, leather, possibly plastic washing-up gloves but
bandits don't like washing-up gloves. They're prone to
tearing and leaving a partial latent, and we can obtain a
match from just one-tenth of a fingerprint. So my guess
would be leather, or cheap plastic. The other glove left a
ridged impression, woollen gloves would leave such a trace.'

'Two men . . . two young men.' The woman seemed to
Yellich to be eager to please, grateful to have company.
She was dressed in a lightweight, canary-yellow summer
dress, with black shoes. She had rings on her fingers and
though she was slight of build and had hands gnarled with
arthritis, her blue eyes sparkled. Yellich liked her.

'Two men?'

'Yes.'

'Young? Old?'

'Young, jeans and T-shirts and those shoes that runners
wear.'

'Trainers . . . and this was when?'

'A couple of days ago.'

'Did you recognize them?'

'No. I've never seen them before but I don't spend my time sitting at the window looking through my net curtains. I read a lot, that's how I pass my time.'

'I see.'

'Just that I was watering my plants, happened to look up and saw them leave the common entrance. Walked away quite slowly, carried a plastic bag, a white bag, like the ones you get from supermarkets – that sort of size, not a large black bin liner.'

'I see.' Yellich pondered the description. So far the lady had not provided any information he felt he needed to take note of. Everything she had thus far told him he could retrieve from memory.

'Looked, a bit like Laurel and Hardy,' the woman volunteered, 'or like Jack Sprat and his wife.'

'You mean one large and one small?'

'Yes. Well, small is wrong . . . average height but one was slightly built the other was well built.'

'That's quite useful. Thank you.'

'Is it?'

'Sounds like a conspicuous pair of individuals. Did you see where they went when they left the building?'

'To a van . . . a small van, had writing on the side.'

Yellich's heart thumped. 'Do you recall what it said?'

The woman smiled. 'Shame on me if I didn't. It said "Fordham Van Hire".' The woman smiled. 'Ought to remember that: I was Betty Packer until I was twenty-one, when I became Betty Fordham. We were together for fifty years. Jack died only last year. I moved into this flat, smaller, better for me now I'm by myself.'

'Fordham Van Hire,' Yellich repeated, and that information he did write in his notebook, and underneath he wrote 'Laurel and Hardy'.

*　　*　　*

Fordham Van and Car Hire revealed itself to be a small part of a larger repair garage which also had a shop attached for 'Motorist's Goods'. It stood on the edge of the city of York near Tadcaster Road at Woodthorpe. A large housing estate was being constructed in the fields adjacent to 'The Fordham Garage'. The garage itself was clearly busy: mechanics toiled on or under cars; on the forecourt, cars waited to be collected by their owners or awaited the attention of a mechanic. It was clearly a place to bring one's car, so observed Yellich as he halted the vehicle against the kerb outside the garage.

'Seems so.' Hennessey saw what Yellich meant. A busy garage is a healthy garage, a business built up on a solid reputation. Word of mouth – the best advertising any small business can have.

The two officers walked from their car to the garage, across the forecourt and into the 'shop'. A young and eager-to-please mechanic gave them directions to 'the boss'.

'The boss' was a well-built, clean-shaven man, dressed in a boiler suit, sitting in front of an untidy desk. A calendar showing a vintage Rolls-Royce outside a stately home hung on the wall behind him. To his side was a battered green filing cabinet, which seemed to Hennessey to be older than the garage itself, as if acquired second-hand when the business was started and still giving sterling service. Hennessey and Yellich, having accepted the invitation to sit down, explained the reason for their visit.

'Well . . .' 'the boss,' Eric Fordham, leaned back in his chair, 'we can certainly let you have access to our records. Sadly, we don't photograph our customers like the large companies sometimes do. That really would have been useful.'

'Certainly would.'

'I don't deal with the van and car hire. Two or three days ago, you said?'

'We think . . . Could go back four days just to spread a wider net?'

Eric Fordham picked up the phone on his desk and dialled a two-figure number. 'It's Eric here.' He grinned at Hennessey and Yellich as he said, 'I have two of York's finest with me, seeking our assistance. Can you bring the van hire book over here, please? Yes, just the vans . . . thanks.' He replaced the phone. 'Tom will be over in a moment, she's a good lass, she'll be as quick as she can.'

'Tom? She?' Hennessey asked.

Thomasina. She was born in Stornoway, way up in Scotland. She told us once that the old habit . . . custom, I mean . . . is to give children names before they were born in the expectation that it would be a male and then to feminize it if that should be necessary. So there are a lot of Fredas, Edwinas, Thomasinas and Donaldinas up there and other similar names, so she said. So, one of our vans has been involved in a felony?'

'Can't really say.' Hennessey shifted in his seat. The hard, unupholstered chair was beginning to get uncomfortable. 'At this stage, all we want to do is trace two youths who were seen driving away from a crime scene a few days ago, if indeed they were driving away from the crime scene at all. We had two witnesses from six flats on a common stairway in Tang Hall, one of whom reported two youths walking to one of your vans and driving away with it. Our Scenes of Crime Officers have determined that two persons were at the crime scene, so we're more than a little anxious to speak to these two young gentlemen if we can trace them.'

'That I can well understand. Did the witness say what type of van it was? We have a mixed fleet . . . Leyland Sherpas and Ford Transits . . . that would narrow it down.'

'Unfortunately she didn't,' Yellich replied, and I didn't think to ask her. Mind, she was . . . is . . . an elderly lady and I don't think she'd be able to easily distinguish one from the other. She'd be of the "all vans look the same to me" school but it'd be worth a re-visit if we didn't get a result here.'

There was a knock on the door. A tall, red-headed woman entered, holding a ledger. She was dressed smartly in a green trouser suit and was in her early twenties. She seemed to Yellich to thrill to male company and Hennessey detected a confidence about her that seemed to stem from the knowledge that she was found attractive by men and he thought: Enjoy it while it lasts, pet.

'This is the rental ledger for the vans.' She handed the ledger to Eric Fordham. She smiled at the two officers. She spoke with a strong Yorkshire accent.

'You deal with the rentals, Tom?' Hennessey asked.

'Yes . . . just me.' She had, he thought, a warm manner as if her all-male, save her, working environment suited her admirably.

'We are keen to trace two men who might have hired a van in the last few days . . . say the last four days – one slightly built, one heavily built . . .'

'Like Laurel and Hardy,' Yellich added.

'Doesn't ring any bells but only one person could have picked up the van and they could have been passengers. There could have been a third person who hired it and picked up Laurel and Hardy.'

'Good point.' Hennessey and Yellich glanced at each other.

'That would be possible if it was a Transit,' Eric Fordham offered. The Sherpas have only one passenger seat, the Ford Transits have a bench seat capable of accommodating two passengers.'

'Definitely a revisit to that witness.' Yellich said.

'They could have used it if someone else hired it,' Thomasina added. 'It's illegal, the insurance is null and void if they do that, but it happens from time to time and we can't stop it, only hear about it if the vehicle is involved in an accident.'

'Another good point,' Hennessey growled, as he felt that this particular promising lead was getting less promising by the minute. 'Anyway, if we could look at the ledger. You haven't computerized?'

'No time for the damn things.' Eric Fordham handed the ledger to Hennessey as Thomasina quietly turned and withdrew.

'Thought you said she was Scottish,' Hennessey said when the young woman was beyond earshot.

'She is. Left Stornoway when she was a babe in arms. Her parents settled in York, where she learned to walk and talk. We go back up there once a year so she can connect with her roots.'

'We?'

'She is my old lady,' Fordham smile. 'The better half, the trouble and strife . . . 'er indoors . . .'

'Ah . . .' Hennessey returned the smile and opened the file. 'Been busy, I see.'

'Yes, happily. The car and van hire bit is doing well. Six vans . . . all six are out right now and I don't think one has been idle for the last week or two.'

'Not according to this log, all hires for the day . . . one for two days.'

'Yes, we don't do half-day hire, we tried that, it didn't work. Folk would hire for half a day and the job would take them past midday so they'd have to pay for a full day's hire and the folk who had hired a van for the afternoon had to manage with whatever vehicle we could scrounge for them. So full-day hire is the minimum . . . no maximum period.'

'No maximum?'

'Nope.' Fordham smiled. 'You can hire a van for six

months if you like and some companies hire for that length of time. Individuals though, they rarely hire for longer than two days'

'As I see . . . so, six vans . . . we'll go back four days, one out for two days, so twenty-one names, twenty-one addresses.' He slid the ledger across to Yellich. 'Rank has its privileges, Sergeant. If you could copy the names into your notepad,' said in good humour.

'Yes, boss,' said with equal good humour.

Hennessey and Yellich returned to Micklegate Bar police station via Sixth Avenue, Tang Hall, and the home of Mrs Fordham. Leaving Hennessey sitting in the car, Yellich walked to Mrs Fordham's flat and returned a few moments later, looking bemused.

'Well, skipper –' Yellich slid into the driver's seat – 'I should know by now not to underestimate anyone. The two young men—'

'Mr Laurel and Mr Hardy?'

'The very same. They got into the front passenger door, one after the other. It was a Transit, she said, without any prompting from me.'

Hennessey chuckled.

'I never would have thought it.' Yellich started the car. 'I mean, how many little old widowed ladies in their seventies would know a Sherpa from a Transit?'

'Not many.' Hennessey indeed thought it a remarkable observation on the part of Mrs Fordham. 'Narrows the list.'

'Down by half . . .'

'Yes.' Yellich drove away. 'I put a "T" beside the names that hired the Transit, all other names hired a Sherpa. So we'll give the names with the "T" beside it priority.'

'Were they all local addresses, do you recall?'

'Yes, boss. All local.'

'Good. You know how much I hate driving, and probably why . . .'

'You did tell me once . . . I'm sorry.'

'Long time ago . . . but I'll stay local, I'll visit the addresses, especially the ones we know, if any, see what criminal records tell us about any of them. You, you can take a trip over to Leeds.'

'To Armley Prison?'

'Yes, see what Shane Sledge can tell us about his brother.'

Yellich parked the car in the car park at the rear of Micklegate Police Station and he and Hennessey entered the building by the 'staff only' entrance, signed as being 'in' and checked their pigeonholes. In Hennessey's pigeonhole was a memo from the Divisional Press Officer requesting an update on the Jane Seymour murder, the press officer having had a number of queries from the media about the case. 'Not much,' Hennessey said to himself, 'apart from the fact that by coincidence she shared the same name as Henry the Eighth's third wife.'

'Sorry, boss?' Yellich turned to him as he leafed through the contents of his own pigeonhole.

'Nothing . . . it's just a query here about the Jane Seymour case. The media is clamouring for progress. Nothing to add. Charles visited with the children over the weekend, chatted about it with him. He pointed out that by coincidence Jane Seymour was the name of the third wife of Henry the Eighth.'

'Really? Beheaded or divorced?'

'Neither. Died of complications following childbirth.'

Hennessey walked down the corridor to his office and recorded the visit to Fordham's Garage in the still thin file of the murder of Gary Sledge. He then signed out of the building and strolled the walls amid throngs of tourists to Lendal Bridge, crossing over the blue and inviting-looking Ouse, upon which a young man in a single scull picked his way among the pleasure craft. A horse-drawn carriage passed him, carrying two parents and their excited children, driven by a coachman in a top hat and scarlet coat. An open-topped double-decker bus crawled patiently behind the coach. Hennessey weaved through the crowds, past buskers and street performers of varying skills, and the inevitable young beggar with a dog on the end of a piece of string, sitting in front of a bowl in which was propped a sign which read: 'Hungry and homeless, please help.' From Stonegate he walked into the Starre Inne, reputedly the oldest pub in York, and accessed by a snickelway which drove narrowly at ninety degrees from the street.

Inside the pub he ordered a meal of Cumberland sausage in onion gravy, which he ate sitting snugly in a corner seat under a large print of a map which had the legend 'The West Ridinge of Yorkshyre with the moft famous and fayre Citie Yorke defcribed. 1610'. Feeling refreshed and good about himself after a satisfying lunch, he strolled back to Micklegate Bar Police Station, once again taking the wall from Leman Street to Micklegate Bar, glancing to his left as he walked, to the area of York known as 'within the walls', where, it is reputed, there is a pub for every day of the year and a church for every Sunday. Reaching Micklegate Bar Police Station he entered by the front, public entrance, nodded to the uniformed constable who was manning the desk and was having trouble giving directions to an agitated Italian tourist. He entered the CID corridor and sat at his desk. He was joined almost immediately by DS Yellich, who rapped on the door frame as he entered Hennessey's office.

'Good lunch, boss?'

'Very good. I assume you went to the canteen. Don't know how you can stand that swill.'

'It's cheap and filling, that's good enough for me.' He brandished a bundle of papers. 'These came back from

C.R. over lunch, sir. Three of the people who hired Ford Transit vans from Fordham's Garage are known to us.'

'Really? Take a pew, let's see what we've got.'

'Well –' Yellich sat down in the chair in front of Hennessey's desk – 'of the three that hired Transit vans and are known to us, I would draw your attention to this guy.' He handed Hennessey a sheet of paper.

'Christopher Kingston.' Hennessey read the name. 'Why he?'

'Well as you see he's in his twenties, same age as the two men seen leaving the house on Sixth Avenue, and he has convictions for violence.'

'Assault, robbery, criminal damage, has served time . . . just out of Armley. That's either a coincidence or it's not.'

'My thoughts exactly, boss, and look at his home address.'

'Tang Hall, Coniston Drive.'

'Hardly a hop and a skip away from Gary Sledge's house.'

'I see why you feel him suspicious, Yellich.'

'Not only that, but the other two are out of the age group, both in their fifties. One known for breaching a court order, and charged with kidnap.'

'Kidnap!'

'Yes, he snatched his own son because he didn't agree with the court's decision to award custody to his ex-wife. He was fined.'

'Lenient.'

'Yes . . . but not known to us before or since.'

'OK, not on our list of suspects, probably have to visit him but only if we don't get anywhere with Mr Kingston.'

'The other fellow, Julian Dodd, he was done for fraud. Again, non-violent, though I dare say he might have picked up a few tricks during the five years he spent as a guest of Her Majesty, and again, not known to us before or since.'

'So . . . we come back to Mr Kingston.' Hennessey glanced at his watch. 'I'll go and visit him.'

'Alone, sir? You don't know what you're walking into.'

'No, I'll take a constable with me. You . . . you drive over to Leeds, have a chat with Shane Sledge and drop Kingston's name. There might be more of a connection there than just the same address until a matter of weeks ago.'

'Very good, boss.' Yellich stood.

Hennessey drove out to Tang Hall, a passenger in a marked police vehicle, a van with 'Dog Section' written on the side, it being the only available vehicle in the car pool. A strongly built constable in his thirties drove. Hennessey had seen the constable in the police station before, but had never spoken to the man. It transpired that he was called Hewitt, was married, and lived in Selby, just outside in fact, little place called Carlton. Beyond that, he proved himself to be a man of few words.

Christopher Kingston was a short but muscular man in his twenties as his record sheet had indicated. He wore only a pair of badly faded jeans, being barefoot and barechested. His hands and arms were covered in self-inflicted tattoos. He had an earring in his left ear, a thin mouth, and piercing, Hennessey thought, cold eyes. He stood square on to the two much larger police officers like a terrier standing up to two Rottweilers, knowing he was going to take the second prize but determined to go down fighting. 'What now?' he snarled, but Hennessey detected a look of worry creeping into the cold eyes, a further paling of the already sickly, pale 'Tang Hall tan'. He thought Yellich's shrewd detective work was going to pay dividends.

'Christopher Kingston?' Hennessey asked.

'Yes.'

'DCI Hennessey. I'd like to have a few words with you.'

'About?'

'About the murder of Gary Sledge.'

Kingston looked stunned. His facial expression said, 'Here already? How did you know?' but he remained silent.

'I think you'd better let us in, a police car outside your house doesn't mean anything but I called on Mr and Mrs Sledge yesterday, and visited Gary Sledge's flat as well. I'll be recognized as the interested police officer and if I'm seen standing on your threshold, the Sledges will find out, they'll visit you and they won't be nice and polite like me and Constable Hewitt here, they'll use claw hammers and pliers and long iron bars to ensure your co-operation. You understand, I think?'

Kingston stepped aside. His flat, like Gary Sledge's, said to Hennessey and Hewitt, as they 'read' it, young man living alone. It was untidy, unclean, hard-looking, functional. Smelled unpleasantly at that moment in the heat of a summer, and was probably cold and difficult to heat during the winter months.

'So what do you want to know?' Kingston asked as he and Hennessey and Hewitt stood in a circle in the middle of the living room, on a carpet which looked to Hennessey to be new, but was already sticky underfoot.

'Anything you can tell us.'

Kingston shrugged his shoulders. He turned and reached for a packet of 'nails', selected one and lit it with a disposable lighter that he held in trembling hands. A lovely, lovely nervous reaction, thought Hennessey, who realized Kingston was a young man with reason to fear the police, if not in respect of the murder of Gary Sledge, then for something.

'You hired a van from Fordham's Van and Car Hire. Three days ago, was it?'

'So what?'

'What did you use it for?'

'Had some furniture to shift.'

'From where to where?'

'A mate was moving house. I helped him.'

Hennessey smiled, as he thought how Kingston's years in youth custody, when he doubtless decorated himself with a pin and a ball of cotton wool saturated with ink, and the years in adult prison hadn't taught him a great deal: never provide an alibi.

'So who was the friend and where did you move from and where did you move to?'

'Just some bloke I know.'

'Name?'

'Just a guy.'

'You don't provide us with his name and you're moving well into the frame for the murder of Gary Sledge.'

Kingston drew heavily on the 'nail' and exhaled through his nose. He remained silent.

'Be happier at the police station, Chris? Do your mates call you Chris?'

Kingston nodded.

'Okay, Chris, you're between a rock and a hard place. You've got to decide whether you're more frightened of the police and a life stretch or the Sledge family.'

Kingston sat, sank down on to the settee . . . 'I'm only out a few weeks . . . now I'm going back in. You've got to protect me from the Sledges.'

'All you need, Chris.'

'There's more than just Gary's father on Fourth Avenue, he's got two brothers, they've all got sons and there's not a softy among them.'

'Who were your mates, one big one and one small one, who were seen walking away from Gary Sledge's house carrying something in a plastic bag and who got into a can marked "Fordham's Van and Car hire"?'

Kingston's head slumped forward. 'So that's how you traced me.'

'Yes. So who were they, the Laurel and Hardy duo?'

Kingston shook his head. 'No names, I'm not grassing anybody up. You've got me. That's all I'm giving up. Just me.'

'Alright. Christopher Kingston, I am arresting you in connection with the murder of Gary Sledge. You do not have to say anything but it may harm your defence if you do not mention when questioned, something which you later rely on in court. Anything you do say may be given in evidence.' Hennessey turned to the constable. 'Can you phone for an escort, please? There's not room for three in the dog van.'

'Sledge.' Shane Sledge accepted the cigarette offered by Yellich. 'It's not a common name in Yorkshire, but it's not uncommon either. A lot of boys get called "hammer" at school because of it but lose the nickname when they leave school, but Gary kept his. He like being called "Hammer", helped his "hard man" image.'

'You don't seem a typical Sledge, Shane.'

Shane smiled. 'I'm not as hard as my Dad would like me to be and when I got banged up, my uncle Robert sent me a postcard saying "about time too".'

Yellich smiled. 'You sound like the good apple, the white sheep of the family.'

'Possibly, but I'm doing time, keeping the family tradition alive. Any news yet, I mean about Gary's murder?'

'Chasing a few leads.' Yellich sat back in the chair in the agents' room of Armley Prison. He found it cramped and cold. Even in high summer it seemed to have a chill about it. There was no source of natural light. 'So what do you know about a youth called Kingston, Christopher Kingston?'

'Kingston! He was here until a week or two ago.'

'We know.'

'Did he have anything to do with Gary's murder?'

'We don't know. Right now he's just a name on a very long list of names.'

Shane Sledge shook his head. 'Kingston, he's not as hard as he'd like to think he is. He wouldn't go up against our family; he left me alone in here. He wasn't frightened of me, I'm just not what Gary used to be, but he was frightened of our family. He'd be frightened of Gary though, he wouldn't go up against Gary and there's no cause . . . I mean, no reason, what's that word?'

'Motive?'

'Yeah, there's no motive. I mean, we know Kingston and he knows us, there's never been anything between us, good or bad.' Shane Sledge was a ginger-haired, well-set young man. He didn't seem to Yellich to be suited to prison life, yet he nevertheless seemed to be taking his time in gaol in his stride. 'No, can't see Kingston doing anything to harm our Gary . . . not Kingston.'

'Well, my boss is chatting with him now. We'll see what he says.' Yellich paused. 'Now, Gary's flat was turned over . . . not burgled, items of value were left. It was as if someone was looking for something. Do you know what it was?'

'I don't.' Shane shook his head.

'You'd tell us if you knew?'

'Yes. I want you to catch the people who did this.'

'Well, possibly you would, Shane, and I believe you but you yourself have mentioned your family . . . your father, your Uncle Robert and you have another uncle . . .'

'Harry.'

'Harry. Three blokes and they all have sons and daughters, all likely to take the law into their own hands. It'll just be worse for them if they do.'

'They're visiting tomorrow. I'll ask them but I don't think they'll listen.'

'OK, if you'd ask anyway. Got a couple more questions for you. Did your brother keep any money in his flat?'

'A few thousand quid, he kept it in a cardboard box.'

'We wondered what was in the box. The box is still there, its contents are not.'

Shane Sledge flushed with anger. 'They'd torture him then shoot him for a couple of thousand quid?'

'We don't think that happened, Shane. Somebody was looking for something in your brother's flat. They probably came across the money and helped themselves, that's what is likely to have happened, which brings me on to the next question. At the time that Gary's flat was turned upside down, two lads, lads about your age, were seen walking from the flat to a van which was driven away by a third person. These lads carried a plastic bag which I suspect contained the few thousand pounds that Gary kept in the cardboard box. They were described as looking like Laurel and Hardy, one big, one small. Any idea who they might have been?'

'Yes, they live on the Hall. Sydney Burton, he's the big one and the little one is Jeff Stafford. They're mates of Kingston's.' He paused. 'So maybe Kingston did have to do with it after all.'

'Possibly.' Yellich wrote the two names in his notepad. 'But do what you can to persuade your family not to do anything rash. Do you know where we can find Burton and Stafford?'

'In your computer. I don't know their addresses but they've got form, plenty of form, particularly Stafford . . . he's the brains, he's sly and cunning. They call him "the Fox", or "Foxy" . . . "Foxy Jeff", "Foxy Stafford". "Big Burton", he's just a lump of putty, useful bit of weight in a fight but that's all he's good for.'

'Alright. Finally, if you can't tell us what your brother had that someone else wanted badly enough to kill him for, do you know who could? A friend . . . a girlfriend?'

'Ask Andy Styles. You'd think he and Gary were brothers, not me and Gary. You'll find Andy's address the same place you'll find Big Burton and Foxy Stafford's addresses. You could talk to Heather Lyall. I don't know how close she and Gary were but he was more serious about her than any other lass he'd known.'

'She'll have a record too?'

'Shoplifting . . . receiving . . . nice girl. I thought she and Gary were well suited. You'll have her address too.'

It was Friday 16.30 hours.

Three

in which a confession is freely given.

'One looks relieved.' Yellich swilled his tea in the mug he held, on which was written 'York Railway Museum' in gold letters on a blue background. 'Another looks bemused, and the third, the third looks angry.'

'Let me guess, Kingston, Burton and Stafford in that order.' Hennessey sipped his tea. He glanced at the small window in his office and noted again how warmly the white/grey walls of the ancient city glowed in the early evening sun.

'Bang on, boss. Kingston sees this as protective custody and, from what we know about the Sledge family, he's probably correct to think like that.'

'I'll say.'

'And Big Burton looks as though he doesn't know what's happening and expects to be able to walk home for his supper any time now and Foxy Stafford looks as if he is planning an escape. So how do you want to handle it, skipper?'

Hennessey leaned forward and intertwined his fingers. 'Well, I want to do it by the book, according to P.A.C.E.'

'Yes, sir.'

'So we need a duty solicitor, get them lawyered up.'

'Very good, sir, I'll get on to that.'

'Could be late working, Yellich.'

'That's alright, sir. Sara will understand. I'll phone her, let her know I'll be late.'

'Good man.'

'So how do we handle it?'

'Weakest first, I say.'

'That would be either Burton or Kingston. Burton because, well, he's there but only just, Kingston because he's frightened stupid of the Sledges.' Hennessey paused. 'You think Burton is borderline mentally subnormal?'

'Learning difficulties, sir, these days it's called "learning difficulties". That's what our Jeremy has.'

'Oh . . .' Hennessey's hand went to his head. 'Somerled, I meant you no harm. I am sorry, that's going on my guilt pile. I'll squirm in years to come when I remember that. I do apologize.'

'No worries, skipper. But Burton's got more about him than our Jeremy's got. Burton might even have been able to survive in a mainstream school, which is something our Jeremy couldn't manage. If we give Jeremy everything we can, he might achieve a mental age of about twelve and be able to cope with semi-independent living in a hostel.'

'Yes . . . good for you.'

'Well, it's like a different and new world opening up to us, sir, and he gives so much to us. Sara gets frustrated at times, especially now, school holidays.'

'So she'll want you home as soon as, tonight?'

'Yes, sir. It won't go down too well that I am not coming home on time tonight but like I said, she'll understand and it's after five p.m. He can watch television, that keeps him quiet.'

'That's the rule is it?' Hennessey smiled. 'No television until after five p.m.?'

'It's what the educational psychologist recommends.

Stimulation during the day: he has books and building blocks and such like. Television doesn't stimulate, but sometimes it's hard for Sara not to give in and let him have the television on during the day to keep him calm and quiet when she is exasperated.'

'I can see the difficulty.'

'Well, it's the way of it at the moment. Jeremy is learning that television can be a reward for bad behaviour. We are trying to avoid sliding down that path.'

'Like people giving children wine to make them sleep and wondering why they become alcoholics.'

'Exactly . . . television during the day is a short-term solution which will lead to a long-term problem. If he's allowed to associate bad behaviour with reward and his own way, we'll never get him into a semi-independent living hostel and if we do, he'll find the adjustment difficult. So, Burton or Kingston?'

'What do you think?' asked Hennessey.

'Well, Burton, I'd say, sir. He's not fully "learning difficulties", he won't need a guardian as dictated by P.A.C.E. should he have been a "vulnerable person". I think he's just this side of that line. I'm sure the solicitor will stop things getting out of hand.'

'Alright, Burton first.'

'I'll phone for a duty solicitor.' Yellich stood.

'Thanks . . . and please apologize to Sara for me. Tell her I'm keeping you.'

'Will do, sir. Thanks.'

The red light glowed, indicating the tape recorder was on. The twin spools were visible, each turning slowly, mesmerically.

'The time is 19.32 hours, the place is Interview Room Two, Micklegate Bar Police Station, York. The date is July 10th. I am Detective Chief Inspector Hennessey.

I am now going to ask other persons in the room to identify themselves.'

'Detective Sergeant Yellich, Micklegate Bar Police Station.'

'Harriet Bush of Wheeler and Perkins, duty solicitor present to represent Mr Burton in accordance with the Police and Criminal Evidence Act 1984.' Harriet Bush was a young woman with sharp features, a little too sharp, thought Hennessey, verging on the waif-like, he felt. She was, he observed, smartly dressed in a pinstripe jacket and skirt, dark nylons, black shoes with a modest heel. He noted metal round her wrist and neck, and rocks upon her fingers. She sat behind a notepad, as if for protection, with a gold ballpoint poised at the ready.

The room fell silent.

'Your name?' Hennessey prompted Burton. 'State your name for the benefit of the tape, please.'

'Me . . . ? Oh . . . Sydney Burton.'

'Your age, Sydney?'

'Twenty-two.'

'And your address?'

'10, Tenth Avenue, Tang Hall. Can't forget that address. That's York, YO31.'

'Thanks. We don't need the postcode just now.'

'Are you employed?'

'No . . . unemployed. Never had a job, really.' Sydney Burton looked confused. Hennessey saw a youth who was snapping out of the attitude that Yellich had described him as having. Now he seemed less sure of being allowed to go home for his supper, now he seemed pale, wide eyed; worry was creeping on. Hennessey saw a large but not particularly muscular boy, rounded shoulders, a stomach which protruded under a tight-fitting red T-shirt, just a plain red shirt, no logo, no trim, just plain like, he thought, Burton himself.

'Do you know why you are here, Sydney?'

'Don't answer that.' Harriet Bush turned to Burton. Her voice was soft yet authoritative. She turned to Hennessey. 'Leading question.'

'I don't think that it is actually.' Hennessey leaned forward. 'It invites more than one answer.'

'It invites Mr Burton to implicate himself.' Harriet Bush avoided eye contact. 'On that basis it is a leading question. Under the rules of the Police and Criminal Evidence Act, it is for the police to state the reason for this interview of my client. I ask you to reword the question. P.A.C.E. is quite specific on this matter.'

'Very well.' Hennessey collected his thoughts. 'Sydney Burton, you are going to be asked questions about the murder of Gary Sledge a.k.a . . .'

'A.k.a.?' Bush stepped in. 'No abbreviations, or initials.'

'Also known as "Hammer". You are not bound to answer but what you do say will be taped and may be given in evidence. Do you understand?'

'Yes.'

'Did you know Gary Sledge?'

'Yes.'

'In what capacity?'

'Capacity?'

'Well, friend, neighbour, old school mate . . . enemy.'

'Oh, just knew him, he lived on the Hall, he was one of the Sledges. So everyone knew him because we all knew the Sledges, but he wasn't a special mate.'

'I see.'

'You know he was murdered?'

'Yes.'

'How do you know he was murdered?'

'Because I was there.'

The silence in the room could be heard. Harriet Bush stiffened as she realized the uphill task that lay ahead of her. Hennessey and Yellich glanced at each other and raised their eyebrows, as in turn they realized the joy of the downhill slope that lay ahead of them. This was going to be one of the easy ones. From the discovery of the corpse to charging the perpetrator, all wrapped up in less than forty-eight hours.

'Didn't have nothing to do with it, though. Didn't know he was going to be killed.'

'Be careful what you say.' Harrier Bush turned to Burton.

'That's good advice to give your client, Miss Bush.' Hennessey leaned back in his chair. 'But the old rule also holds good here.'

'What, pray, is the particular rule to which you refer? The "old rule", what rule is that? This interview is to be conducted under the rules of P.A.C.E. Nothing else.'

'The old unwritten rule: the more your client helps us, the more he helps himself.'

'You can't plea-bargain. It's not allowed in the United Kingdom.'

'I know. But what evidence your client gives in the witness box, and his guilty plea to what, in our discretion, we charge him with, will be reflected in his sentence.'

Harriet Bush paused. 'It's in your interest to co-operate, depending on what evidence can be mustered against you.' She spoke to Burton. 'This officer has mentioned one unwritten rule. I mention another, "Cough to nowt".'

'Cough to nowt?' Burton echoed.

'Admit to nothing.'

'Very well. Let's inch forward.' Hennessey glanced at his watch. 'We've got more than twenty-two hours left before we have to charge you or let you go.'

'I could be here all night?'

'Oh yes.' Hennessey held eye contact. 'Not only could you be in custody until well after tomorrow, but you could be in custody for the next twenty-five years. Accessory to murder, either before or after the fact, carries the same sentence, which in the UK can mean anything from five years to drawing your last breath behind bars and anything in between. Last few years will be easy, they'll be spent in the "Grey House".'

'Grey House?'

'A prison in southern England for all non-dangerous convicts over the age of fifty. Being an accessory to murder doesn't make you a dangerous prisoner, it's your conduct inside which determines whether you are dangerous or not. So, tell us what happened.'

Burton glanced at Harriet Bush, who shook her head – 'say nothing'. Then she turned to Hennessey and said, 'My client declines to comment.'

'With respect, Miss Bush, your client has admitted to being present at the murder. We have evidence to show that the deceased was not just deprived of food and fluid for a day or two before he died but that he was tortured. That means he was held against his will and that means the murder was premeditated. The concept of manslaughter won't come into this. This is premeditated murder. So we are talking about abduction, false imprisonment, serious assault, premeditated murder.' Hennessey drew his breath. 'So, Mr Sledge was not released from his false imprisonment, he was murdered during it. His release was his death, his murder. Your client is now on record –' Hennessey pointed to the slowly turning cassettes – 'as admitting he was present at the murder. That means he was present during Mr Sledge's imprisonment, his unlawful imprisonment.'

Harriet Bush looked shaken.

'You see, Sydney, Chris Kingston admits to hiring a van from Fordham's van hire. You and Foxy Stafford fit the description of two boys seen walking away from Gary Sledge's flat after it had been turned over as if someone was looking for something, but what you did take was a few thousand pounds that Gary Sledge kept under his bed. If we find it in your flat—'

'I live with me mum.'

'Or in Foxy Stafford's flat.'

'He lives with his parents too.'

'No matter, we'll get a warrant to search both. Tell us, where will we find it? So we don't have to make the sort of mess in your mum's house that you made in Gary Sledge's.'

'It's under my bed in an old biscuit tin.'

Another pause.

'I would like to confer with my client.' Harriet Bush spoke once again, softly, but with a degree of authority.

Hennessey reached for the stop button. 'It is now 20.09 hours. The interview is terminated to allow Mr Burton to consult with his legal representative.' Hennessey switched off the tape recorder. He and Yellich stood. 'I'll have a constable bring some refreshment in for you both.'

The room smelled heavily of furniture polish. The man was lean, hungry-looking, like Cassius. As soon as he'd come in and set eyes on him, he thought, Cassius. If I were to cast *Julius Caesar* . . .

'There's been a development.' He spoke nervously and eyed the two 'heavies' who stood either side and a little behind the man, sinister, he thought, in casual clothes, not dark-suited muscle as in the Hollywood films. This man's minders wore jeans and T-shirts and trainers, like any student would wear, except these two were not peace-loving students. They looked like wrestlers and their bodies rippled with hard-packed muscle.

'Oh.' The man, cold-eyed, inclined his thin face towards the man who had called on him unannounced, and in the evening, which the man regarded as his 'golden time'.

Some folk enjoy the mornings but he, he, always different, particularly enjoyed the evenings between six and nine. 'What development?'

'The police have arrested three of the lads.'

The man remained expressionless.

'Well, they've taken them in for questioning.'

'As good as. Just three?'

'Yes.'

'What about the other two?'

'Keeping their heads down. They're scared of the Sledge family, see, but so far their names aren't linked.'

'What happens if they are linked?'

'The Sledges will kill them.' He looked beyond the man out over the vast lawn, the neatly tended border, the soft fading sky behind, blue, with a streak of crimson, swallows darting hither and thither. The man suddenly valued life.

'This has been a mess.'

'Yes. That boy . . . he didn't know anything.'

'How long did you persuade him for?'

'Twenty minutes . . . half an hour.'

'What!' The man shot to his feet. 'Twenty minutes . . . twenty minutes. You had him for over two days.'

'We thought the hunger would do it.'

'We thought . . . you being you and the other idiot, Silcock.'

'Yes. The lads just did what we told them to do.'

'They don't know about me?'

'No, Mr Hollander.'

'Good.' Hollander smiled a cruel smile. 'They'd better not. But twenty minutes . . . you have to keep the juice flowing until they're bleeding from every orifice . . . hours . . . days. Your problem, Silcock, you know your problem . . .'

'What?'

'You're too soft. You panicked didn't you? Couldn't

stand a little bit of screaming, so you reckoned he wasn't going to give anything up so you panicked and silenced him.'

'Pomfret shot him. He'd done it before. He knew how to do it.'

Hollander shook his head. 'So your problem is you panicked. You know my problem? My problem is that I am worth ten – fifteen million pounds and I still won't spend money. No wonder you came cheap, you're no good, no good at all. I should have spent money and hired a couple of professionals.'

'About the money . . .'

'The money . . . you didn't come up with the goods did you? There's nothing coming to you.'

'But . . .'

'No buts. The problem isn't mine, Silcock – it's yours. Find out what the cops know. If I get fingered, you lose your life, you and Pomfret both. I have "Frostbite", remember?'

When Hennessey and Yellich had resumed their seats in the interview room, and when Hennessey had restarted the tape, stated the time and date and location, and when each person in the room had introduced him or herself, Harriet Bush said, 'My client wishes to make a full confession.'

The tension in the room lifted instantly, and both Hennessey and Yellich relaxed their postures.

'On the understanding that this co-operation will be noted in the court hearing.'

'Well, it won't be ignored. Will Mr Burton testify, voluntarily, also?' Harriet Bush turned to Burton and said, 'It's in your interests, you've dug yourself into a hole, and you should use every means to dig yourself out.'

'I'll need to be looked after.' Burton spoke with a pleading voice, which Hennessey found a trifle pathetic.

'Looked after?'

'Witness Protection,' Harriet Bush explained.

Hennessey nodded. 'That's possible, even if Mr Burton is sent to prison.'

'Prison!' Burton wailed. 'I thought—'

'Think nothing,' Hennessey snapped. 'Prison for you is a possibility, depending on your involvement with this crime, and since the crime is premeditated murder after abduction, false imprisonment and serious assault . . . then you'll be lucky to walk, very lucky. You will, however, be doing much to reduce your sentence and we can hide you in the system. Under the Witness Protection Scheme, we can have you do time away from anyone who knows you, in the South of England, or Scotland, or Wales . . . different name, tell the other cons you're in for burglary, even the screws won't know the truth.'

'Screws?'

'Prison officers, guards. The governor will have to know but the lads on the wing, the hall officers, well, they'll know as much as you want to tell them.'

Burton glanced at Harriet Bush, who said, 'It's still a good idea to co-operate. You're in too deep to do anything else. I'll make sure you don't implicate yourself further.'

'OK.' Burton shrugged.

'Well,' Hennessey spoke softly, 'in your own words, Sydney.'

Sydney Burton looked awkward and kept throwing nervous glances towards Harriet Bush. Eventually he said, 'Well it was Foxy what set it all up.'

'"Foxy"?' That would be Jeffrey Stafford?'

'Yes. "Foxy Stafford" . . . "Foxy Jeff" . . . "Foxy Staffy".'

'OK. So, for the record, by "Foxy" you mean Jeffrey Stafford.'

'Yeah . . . I said.'

'OK. Carry on.'

'Well, we got Chris Kingston to help us.'

'To abduct Gary Sledge?'

'Yeah.'

'Who else was there? How many others?'

'How did you know there were more?'

'I didn't until just now but I guessed. I mean, Stafford is small and weasel like, Kingston is no hard man and you . . . big and heavy on the outside but frankly I think you'll find prison hard going. Some men like fat boys. I don't think you three could take Gary Sledge, especially when you know it's not just him you're up against, but the whole of the Sledge clan. Ever heard of the expression "taking a tiger by the tail"?'

'No.'

'Well, think . . . grab the tail, which is easy to get hold of, the head turns round and gobbles you up. That's what happens if you grab Gary Sledge, any Sledge, off the street, so you need more than you three bantamweights. You'd better tell me.'

'I'm not grassing anymore.'

'You'll be saving their lives. It's a question of who gets to them first, us or the Sledges.' Hennessey paused. 'Not a lot is missed on an estate like Tang Hall, you know that more than me. One of the Sledges has been iced, the police are investigating, we've been seen arresting you and Kingston and Foxy Stafford, and we'll be going back to your drums with search warrants. That'll all be seen, all transmitted back to the Sledges. Anyone associated with you is going to have a member of a very nasty family tapping on their doors and windows with a smile on their face, a crowbar in their hands. There's going to be blood spilled in the Hall tonight unless you start coughing.'

Burton glanced at Harriet Bush, who said, 'I'd tell them, for their sake if not for yours. If you want me to, I'll square it with them, tell them you gave their names to save their lives.' She addressed Hennessey: 'It would be better coming from me.'

'I have no objection to you doing that, Miss Bush.'

'Ernie Diamond and Phil Corr.'

'Have they got form?'

'Bit.'

'So we'll have their addresses.' Hennessey turned to Yellich. 'Can you see to that, please, Sergeant?'

Yellich stood. 'Ernest Diamond and Philip Corr. I'm on it.'

'The tape interview is halted to allow DS Yellich to leave the room.' Hennessey switched the tape recorder off. 'DS Yellich will be back in a few minutes. He won't be making the arrest, he'll despatch two cars to do that.' He stood. 'But I'll leave you two alone for a minute or so.' He exited the room.

Hennessey walked from the interview room corridor, past the cell block and found Yellich in the control room.

'Cars on their way, sir.' Yellich smiled at Hennessey.

'Good. Hope for their sake that they are home.' He glanced at his watch. 'Eight thirty, they'll be off up to the pub soon, especially if Kingston and Burton shared out the money they found under Sledge's bed.'

'It's going to be touch and go, sure enough, more for them than us. I wouldn't like to fall into the clutches of a revenge-seeking Sledge family.'

'Me neither.'

Hennessey and Yellich waited in the control room until the radio crackled and first Michael Zulu Foxtrot and then Michael Tango Delta radioed in reporting, 'Arrests completed.'

Yellich and Hennessey glanced at each other, each wearing a look of relief and thankfulness.

'I'll brief the custody sergeant,' Hennessey said. 'I'll

have them detained under suspicion of conspiracy to murder and have them kept in separate cells. Let them sweat.'

'Very good, boss. I'll see you back in the interview room.'

Silcock and Pomfret knocked nervously on Ernest Diamond's door. There was no answer. All inside was quiet; no artificial light burned despite it being dusk. Silcock knocked again. The only sound was the hollow emptiness of the echo of his knocking. Then the door behind opened, a man in a vest and white slacks stood in the doorway. He looked at Silcock and Pomfret and said, 'The busies lifted him.'

'When?'

'Just a few minutes ago. Heard you banging, thought it was the busies again. White as a sheet he was, more than just burglary this time.'

Silcock and Pomfret looked at each other.

'If they got Diamond, they'll have Corr by now.' Pomfret spoke with a trembling voice.

'So now we are a gang of five.' Hennessey sat down and switched on the tape recorder and once again stated the time and place and then identified himself and asked those present in the room to similarly identify themselves. The hugely important preliminaries completed, he then said, 'Alright, Sydney, we're all ears.'

Sydney Burton glanced round him: the plastered walls painted in two tones of brown, light brown above dark; the parquet floor; the single filament bulb in the ceiling, behind a Perspex frame. 'Well, it was Foxy set it all up. He said a man had asked him for help. We had to roll this guy, lure him into a garage then give him a kicking ... put him down, tie him to a ladder.'

'A ladder?'

'Yes, you know, a ladder. Part of a set of ladders was on the floor of the garage. We had to tie him to the ladders. We used chain in the end, and a few padlocks. So anyway, we said alright because there was going to be a drink in it for us.'

'A drink?'

'Two hundred each.'

'Alright . . .'

'Anyway, then Foxy told us it was Gary Sledge we would be rolling.'

'Who's "we"?'

'Me and Kingston and Foxy Stafford. So me and Chris Kingston said, "No way", we'd need more people if we were going to roll Gary Sledge. So Foxy says, alright, he'll get more, but the drink will be smaller, it'll be nearer £150 apiece. So we said OK.'

'You weren't frightened of being identified by Sledge?'

Burton shrugged. 'I want out of this hole. I thought, 150 quid, that'll get me to London, see a bit of the world, get a flat, start fresh down there.'

'You never read those posters in the unemployment offices, the job centres? Don't go to London unless you have good qualifications or a lot of money, or both, or something like that.'

'It was a hundred and fifty quid.'

'About enough to buy a cup of coffee.' Hennessey watched Burton pale. He thought Yellich was right, the boy was borderline learning difficulties, or to call a spade a spade, he wasn't a spit short of needing someone to tie his shoelaces each morning. 'I'm a Londoner, sunshine, I should know.'

'We got more money.'

'Yes, from under Gary Sledge's bed. When were you going to split?'

'Next week. So was Kingston and the others, we get our Social Security money paid once a fortnight . . . payday next week. We were going to lift our two weeks then go to the station, first train to London and a new life. We would have had about three, four hundred apiece. We thought that would be enough. Kingston said the Sledges wouldn't follow us. Foxy said the same. So me and Diamond and Corr went along with it. Once we were clear of York, we wouldn't be bothered by the Sledges, that's what we thought.'

'We'll leave that for the moment.' Hennessey drew his breath. 'So, you were told to lure Sledge to a garage?'

'Yes.'

'You know the garage?'

'I do now.'

'You'll be able to tell us where it is?'

Burton nodded.

'OK. So how did you do that?'

'Well, Foxy thought it up. He said the Sledges have connections, they can fence stuff.'

'Can they now?' Hennessey glanced at Yellich.

'Interesting.' Yellich held eye contact with Hennessey.

'Yes . . .' Burton continued. Hennessey thought Burton was enjoying the attention. He had seen the like before, the extent that some people will go to give good information in return for attention, especially if the person who is giving the attention is perceived to have a degree of authority or higher level of status. 'Anyway, Foxy told Sledge that he'd been turning windows while Sledge was inside. He'd got rid of a lot of stuff but some he couldn't move. A lot of good-quality jewellery, and a whole box of fifty pound notes, it was the last one that made Sledge's ears prick up, Foxy said.'

'It did?'

'Yeah. Well see, folk, shopkeepers and publicans are

suspicious of fifties – you don't get them from those cash machines outside banks, so either they're forged or people like us, the dole boys, we've stolen them. Can't change them in a bank if they're genuine, 'cos the bank staff will take it off you and ask you to wait and you know they're calling the police, they'll come and want to know where you got it . . . so you run, you lose fifty quid and you're caught on the CCTV, so the police will recognize you and knock on your door, so Foxy said. But Foxy said he was talking to a guy who used one of Gary Sledge's uncles to move a wad of fifties he'd nicked. He got twenty quid for each fifty.'

'Nice profit for someone.'

'Aye, well it was twenty quid for each or burn the lot. The guy who bought them sold them to a bookmaker who gave him forty for each one. So Foxy's mate got twenty for each fifty, the Sledges got twenty, and the bookie got ten.'

'Bookie took the risk and got least. Doesn't seem right.'

'Well, that's what I heard and the bookie didn't pay them all of it at once, it was just a one time thing. The bookie cashed up each day and once a week he slipped a fifty-pound note in with all the rest, not enough for the bank to sit up and look at what was happening, especially if he had accounts with more than one bank and after a year or so he'd got rid of it.'

'I see . . . interesting. The bookie would want more than that but I see how it works, even if your figures are a bit suspect, I understand the scam. Just need a legitimate business which is used to dealing with a lot of ready cash at the end of the chain and which is run by a character who'll bend the rules. So that's what Foxy said to Sledge?'

'I think so.'

'So Sledge thought he could work the same scam probably using the same bookie but first he had to inspect the stash?'

'Leading my client, Mr Hennessey.' Harriet Bush spoke sharply

'Sorry. Carry on, Sydney.'

'Well anyway, Foxy brought Sledge to the garage, opened it up and they stepped in and it was all down to "hit him before he can hit you". There were five of us and one of him but he was still a Sledge, and Gary Sledge at that. He didn't go down easily but he was our ticket out of the Hall, out of York. So we kept hitting, didn't let up until he was still, but we didn't hit his head. Foxy was strong on that point. We hadn't got to hit his head. I reckon he just gave up without passing out as such. Surprised me, that. Anyway, we took his clothes off.'

'You removed his clothing?'

'Yes. Foxy told us to. Then we tied him to the ladder. We wrapped his clothes round his wrists and ankles and then put the chain round the clothing so the chain wouldn't mark the skin.'

'Wait a minute.' Hennessey held up his hand. 'Stafford, "Foxy" Stafford, didn't want the chain to leave markings?'

'No.' Burton shook his head as if in wonderment. 'Didn't know the reason, just did what Foxy said he wanted done.'

'Why did you remove his clothes?'

'Well, he wasn't able to go to the toilet, was he? Foxy didn't want him messing his clothes.'

'That,' Hennessey said dryly, 'was very thoughtful of Foxy.'

'Yes.' Burton smiled. 'Foxy's alright, really, he's looked after me.' Hennessey thought, Looked after you to the point that you're facing a life term – that's some looking after.

'So then what happened? He's unconscious, well tired after the hammering. You chain him to a ladder and remove his clothes . . . then what?'

'Then this guy comes in, older guy . . . guy in his thirties, forties and another two guys.'

'Would you know their names by any remote chance?'

'No, but I think Foxy called one "Pomfret".'

'Pomfret?'

'Sounded like that. The two guys came into the garage and one looked at Foxy and said, "Well done," and Foxy said, "Just as you said, Mr Pomfret." I'm sure it was "Pomfret" he said. Never heard the name before, so I sort of remembered it. Pomfret.'

Hennessey wrote the name on his pad and slid it to Yellich. 'There won't be many Pomfrets in York, be even less in C.R.'

Yellich stood and left the room.

Hennessey said, 'The time is 20.42. DS Yellich has left the room.' He turned to Burton. 'So, Pomfret and another man. Do you know his name?' Burton shook his head vigorously. 'Never got his name.'

'Alright. This is good, Sydney, you are really doing yourself a favour.'

'I am?'

'Yes, you are. So then what?'

'Well, then we were given our wedges. Pomfret, if that was his name, gave a wedge to Foxy and Foxy shared it out, equal shares. Then he told us to come back the next evening and we did. Sledge was still there chained to the set of ladders, looking worried, but no harm was being done. He just was a bit bruised and this guy Pomfret said for us to come back the next evening, same thing, nothing being done, just a bit more bruised. Told us to come back the evening after . . . that would be three nights ago . . .' Burton's voice tailed off.

'Things were different then?'

'How did you know?'

'The way your voice faded, the way your eyes looked distant.'

'Yeah, well, so would yours.'

'So what happened?'

'Guy was wired up. Electric flex wired to both ankles
. . . the other end attached to a car battery with those clips
like you have on jump leads. The other guy kept touching
the battery terminal with the other clip . . . crocodile clips,
I think they're called. When he did that, Sledge, he twisted
and turned and yelled but they had a gag in his mouth so
nothing much came out of his mouth and Pomfret kept
saying, "Where are they? Where are they?" Each time
Sledge shook his head, Pomfret gave him another blast.
Then the other guy turned to Foxy and said, "You got the
van." Foxy said yes and Pomfret pulled a gun, a real gun,
then put it into a plastic bottle, the type that contains
mineral water, rested the empty bottle against Sledge's
head and pulled the trigger. Hardly a sound . . . left a
powder burn, the plastic couldn't prevent that, but no sound
to speak of.'

'Poor man's silencer,' Hennessey commented. 'I have
heard of the like, never come across it before. So then what?'

'Well, then we put Sledge's clothes back on his body
and the other guy, he tells us to take Sledge's body out
and dump it somewhere where it can be found.'

'Can be found?'

Burton looked uncomfortable. 'That's what Foxy said,
but me, I was standing nearer the older guy and I was
sure he said leave it somewhere it *can't* be found. But I
didn't want to argue with Foxy 'cos he always knows
what's what. So we drove into the centre of York. Kingston,
he was all for leaving him on the street outside his dad's
house but Foxy said no to that, said what we'd done was
bad enough. So he drove within the walls and we put him
on this ledge of grass, that was a bit before dawn, then
Foxy took us back to the Hall, dropped us off at his house
and we went in and drank some vodka. I walked home
about ten/eleven o'clock that morning.'

There was a tap on the door. DS Yellich entered and sat next to Hennessey. He handed Hennessey a file.

'The time is 20.54. DS Yellich has re-entered the room.' Hennessey looked at the file Yellich had handed to him. It was on one Raymond Pomfret, then aged forty-one years by his D.O.B. Hennessey turned the file to Burton, and using his notepad to cover written information, he said, 'I am showing Sydney Burton a photograph. I now ask Mr Burton if he recognizes the man shown in the photograph?'

'That's Pomfret,' Burton said, without hesitation. 'That's the guy who shot Sledge.'

It was Friday 20.59 hours.

Four

in which George Hennessey is reminded of the Chief Superintendent's demons and later meets two women, both of whom lament earlier, happier days.

George Hennessey knocked on Chief Superintendent Sharkey's door, waited for the familiar, and what he found somewhat imperious, 'Come!' before entering.

'Ah, George, good morning.'

'It is a pleasant morning indeed, sir.' Hennessey strode confidently into the room. 'You wanted to see me?'

'Yes, George, please take a pew.'

Hennessey settled into the chair in front of Sharkey's all too neatly, in his opinion, kept desk, everything annoyingly 'just so', pens placed to millimetre-exact perfection, and he did so with a heavy heart. He knew what soul-baring confession, what concern for his welfare was coming. It happened, he estimated, about once every six months and he thought it like watching an old film for the umpteenth time, sometimes the dialogue isn't how he remembered it from last time, or the time before that, or still the time before that, but the story is the same.

'Big case just developed?' Sharkey was a sharply dressed man, bristlingly clean, in his early forties, young, very

young for one of such lofty rank, though Hennessey did
not envy him. His own rank at his age suited him to perfection.

'The murder of Gary Sledge? Yes, sir.'

'I checked with the custody sergeant this morning when
I came in. I understand they've all been charged?'

'Well, all that we have arrested, yes, sir. Now they're
on remand in Full Sutton. We tried to pick up Pomfret
but he wasn't at home. We'll knock on his door this
forenoon.'

'Good. So I am not eating into your P.A.C.E. time?'

'No, sir. As I say, all that have been arrested have been
charged ... Magistrate's Court on Monday and we'll
oppose bail. Mind you, I don't think bail will be requested.'

'Oh?'

'No, sir. I think they realize they're safer inside than
out, despite the privations within and the pleasures without.
I must say the lawyer was very good last night, did more
than her job at her own suggestion.'

'Really?'

'Yes, she represented the lad Burton, who isn't quite
the full shilling. Sergeant Yellich doesn't think he's suffi-
ciently deficient to be labelled "learning difficulties" but
not a hop and a skip short of it. He's the sort of fella
who'd survive in mainstream education, but only just, and
would hold down a job lifting things ... like a refuse
collector.'

'I see.'

'Anyway, he gave up the gang when we pointed out to
him that his mates were being hunted by the Sledge tribe,
who rule the roost on Tang Hall. The murdered lad was
one of that family. So we lifted them and charged them.
We had corroborative evidence, van hire records, witness
statements from neighbours, a stash of money in the possession of each, payment for services rendered to Pomfret,

plus what they nicked from Sledge's flat, more, much more than they could acquire legitimately. Anyway, the solicitor, Miss Bush, haven't met her before, she went to see them each in turn and explained to them what Burton had done. It came better from a mouthpiece than from a cop, and when they realized that Burton hadn't given them up to serve his own ends, but done it to save their lives, then, well, then it was safe for Burton to be with them, he didn't have to be put in the vulnerable prisoners' unit.'

'I see. So, you'll be fondling Pomfret's collar. He's . . . ?'

'The guy who hired Burton and his mates to lure Gary Sledge to his death, and it was Pomfret who shot Sledge, so said Burton.'

'So, you've got the minnows?'

'So far, sir.'

'Motive?'

'As yet undetermined, sir, but it seems that Pomfret believed Sledge had something or some things. Burton reported Pomfret repeatedly saying, or demanding, "Where are they?"'

'They?'

'They. That's all he said, apparently. "Where are they?" So two or more of something, which is either animal, vegetable or mineral. Burton wasn't there all the time. On the first day, having secured Sledge to a set of ladders, they left him alone with Pomfret and another guy. So it's certain that Sledge knew what "they" were.'

'Or who?'

'Yes –' Hennessey nodded, as his scalp tightened – 'or who.'

'So where now, George?'

'Quizzing Stafford, Kingston, Diamond and Corr, being the other "minnows" as you call them, which indeed they are. Bringing Pomfret in for a major quiz session, he's got form by the way . . . for fraud.'

'I see.'

'And we have to visit a friend of Gary Sledge's, a youngster called Styles, Andy Styles. Shane Sledge, Gary's brother, he's in Armley at the moment so as to become a fully paid-up member of the clan, though Yellich reports he's not of the same mould as the rest of the Sledges, he told us of Andy Styles . . . said he might know something of interest.'

'I see . . . well . . .' Sharkey sat back. 'The reason I wanted to see you, George, is that I am a little worried.'

'Oh yes, sir.' Hennessey sat forward, though his heart sank at the prospect of the soul-baring he knew was to follow.

'Amateurs,' Hollander snarled. 'I should have hired men who would know what to do.' His voice echoed in the enclosed space. 'The police have lifted those boys. They'll be spilling right now.'

'They don't know your name, Mr Hollander.' Pomfret shook with fear.

'Don't even know ours.' Silcock's voice was equally shaky; he strained against the rope which bound him hand and foot.

Two further men stood in the room. Still, silent, as if awaiting orders.

'Doesn't matter, they soon will, they'll pick up the trail to you two . . . you'll lead them to me.'

'Please,' Pomfret pleaded, 'I've got a family.'

'You had a family.' Hollander glanced at Pomfret, then at Silcock, and then at Pomfret. 'I told you I had "Frostbite", didn't I? Which one of you is going in first?' He pointed to Pomfret. 'You.'

The two heavies stepped forward.

'Used to be the case that the police meant protection, now

it means trouble.' Mrs Pomfret sat on the floor of her living room, not cross-legged, which might indicate some degree of self-determination, self-control, but with her back resting against an armchair and her legs stretched out in front of her, slightly apart. It was, thought Hennessey, a gesture of defeat. 'Used to be the case that Raymond was going somewhere in life. Used to be the case.' She wore faded denim jeans, a T-shirt, too large for her, in glaring orange, which contrasted with the dark colours of the room, the oak furniture, the faded green carpet, the equally faded brown wallpaper. 'Used to be many things.'

'We understand your husband was convicted of fraud?'

Emily Pomfret nodded. 'Used to be things were, well . . . used to be . . . used to be.'

'Do you know where your husband is?'

She shook her head. 'Not these days . . . he comes . . . he goes . . . he doesn't tell me. Sometimes he has money, enough to buy food, pay off a bit of the mortgage but most of the time we're on the dole. My father was a bank manager, my sister married into serious money, but me . . .' She scratched at a patch in the carpet. 'It's easy being poor, you just buy whatever's cheapest. Used to be things were better . . . Used to be Raymond had a job. My father said I shouldn't marry an actor. Anyway, Raymond wasn't an actor, he was a theatre manager. He was the manager of the Cauldron Theatre. Used to put on avant-garde theatre . . . Used to cater for a student audience in the main, a lot of one-man shows. Raymond liked it. We had enough money for the mortgage. I mean it's not much . . . a terraced house in Holgate . . . not many tourists here, but it's nearly ours and it's warm in winter. Used to be things were OK for us, then he puts his silly hand in the till. Not just once, but it got to be a habit, so he was caught. Can't hide from the annual audit man, the bogeyman with the briefcase and the calculator. I didn't know anything about it, but in hindsight . . . suddenly things just started to loosen up. Money was always tight, we'd empty the penny jar and walk down to the Woodman's Arms for a beer or two each and live off cheap cuts of meat and the cheapest tinned food. We'd buy clothes from the charity shops and holidays were unknown. The nearest we got to a holiday was postcards friends sent us from their holidays. Used to be that was what it was like. Then suddenly it changed, suddenly we had a drinks' corner . . . it was over there by the television . . . vodka, whisky, gin, bottles just standing there like a group of soldiers . . . or Raymond would take me for a drink and open his wallet at the bar. Didn't check if he had enough before we went out, just on with the coats and breeze down to the Woodman's Arms like as if money was no object . . . food . . . that started to come from Marks & Sparks and clothing was new. It never occurred to me that Raymond was up to no good, you don't think that of your husband. Then one day the boys in blue knocked on the door. From that moment my life changed, from that moment the police started to mean trouble for us.'

'What does your husband do?' Hennessey found it difficult to breathe within the house, heated, as it was, greenhouse-like.

'I told you, he comes, he goes. He hasn't worked since he came out of prison. He was angry about that . . . going inside. His solicitor said he could hope for probation and an order to repay the money, first offence, no violence involved and as embezzlement went, it was fairly small. There was a woman being tried for the same offence. I don't mean the same offence as in co-accused . . .'

'No . . . no.' Hennessey was content to allow Emily Pomfret to tell her story. Her co-operation, if and when he needed it, would be more readily forthcoming to one who had lent a sympathetic ear, so he believed, so he had learned from previous experience. 'Similar crime?'

'Yes, she was being done for embezzling four or five million from her employers . . . They were merchant bankers. She collected four and a half years – out in two, and if she'd been clever she would have laundered enough to make the two years inside worth it. They rescued more than two million but more than two million was never recovered, but that woman didn't necessarily abuse a position of trust. She was a low-grade employee who used her knowledge of computers to move her employers' money about. Raymond on the other hand . . .'

'Was in a position of trust?' Yellich said as he longed for an open window.

'Yes. He embezzled two or three thousand . . . and collected eighteen months. His solicitor said that's why he was sent down. Not the amount of cash taken, but the abuse of a position of trust involved in the commission of the crime. Used to be we were happy. Used to be I could trust my husband. Now I don't know where he goes or who he goes with or where the money comes from. He comes home with a wad of notes sometimes. I don't ask because I don't want to know. Just grateful to be able to buy some cheap tins of something and give the building society something. Used to be . . .'

'So do you know where your husband is now?'

Emily Pomfret glanced up at the small clock on the cluttered mantelpiece. 'Dunno. Used to be I knew where he was at any given time of the day. Could be anywhere. York isn't a big city but it has plenty of places to hide.'

'Did he mention a name ever? As a person he might be with?'

'Mmmm . . .' Emily Pomfret gazed dreamily round the room. 'There's a man called Silcock, Ian Silcock, they teamed up when he was on the inside.'

'Teamed up? So we'll know him?'

'I suppose. He was a white-collar criminal as well . . . they found each other, Ray and this guy Silcock. "Only decent game of chess I got," Ray said once . . . and he comes from York.'

'Interesting.'

'Well, that's the only bloke I know he might be with. Never brought Silcock home, might still be inside for all I know . . . Silcock, I mean. Why, anyway? Why do you want to speak to Raymond?'

'His name came up.' Hennessey stood. Yellich did likewise. 'We'd be interested in where he got those wads of notes you mention.'

'Particularly since he's not employed.'

'Used to be . . . used to be employed, used to be a theatre manager. Used to be I was the wife of a theatre manager.'

Hennessey and Yellich stepped out into Holgate, across from the corner shop named the 'World Beer Centre', which had figured in an earlier crime successfully investigated by Hennessey and Yellich, though neither remarked on it.

'Well.' Hennessey looked at Yellich. 'Used to be . . .'

'Used to be indeed.' Yellich smiled. 'Used to be many things . . . many things used to be.'

'That phrase is going to annoy me. It's going to stay with me.'

'Me too, boss. No wonder he spends so much time out of the house.'

'Yes. My empty house is quite warm by comparison.'

'So is my stressed little number. So . . . Silcock? It's the next lead. Shall I check with C.R.?'

'If you'd be so kind.' Hennessey took off his Panama and mopped his brow with a handkerchief. 'Roll on autumn,' he said, but Yellich was engrossed with his mobile phone.

Moments later, Yellich said, 'Got a pen and paper, boss?'
Hennessey took out his notepad.

'St Swithin's Walk, Holgate.'

'That's Silcock's address?'

'Yes, boss.'

'That's just round the corner from here.'

'I know. Just down there . . .' Yellich pointed down the twin rows of blackened terraced houses that were Poppleton Street.

'Amazing,' Hennessey said as he and Yellich fell into step, 'two blokes can live so close to each other yet don't meet until they're banged up together.'

'Strange,' Yellich agreed. 'My wife has a similar tale.'

'Really?'

'Yes. She's a teacher . . . or was, if you remember?'

'Yes.'

'Strange tale. She went to two universities, one for her degree in English literature, the other, the second university for her Teaching Certificate . . . her B.Ed, so called.'

'Yes.'

'She met another female student on that course, here at York University, in fact, got on like a house on fire. Anyway, it turns out they had attended the same previous university, which was Lancaster . . . different faculties but the same university. Turned out further that they both came from Liverpool, both attended the same comprehensive school, both had attended the same junior and primary schools and both had grown up in houses on the same street.'

'Heavens.'

'Yep . . . after all that, the first time they met was at their second university and only then because they were in the same tutorial group. She explained that friendships grew out of the tutorial groups . . . one or two marriages as well. So if they had been in different tutorial groups they might still not have met. Sara says it feels as though they were destined not to meet and that they had cheated destiny.'

'Sounds like it.'

'They're still friends and when she and her husband visit, nobody and nothing comes between them, me and her husband just don't get a look in. She came over earlier this summer when her husband had taken their children out for the day to give her a break, brought a bottle of wine with her and she and Sara sat outside from three p.m. to eight p.m., leaving me with Jeremy. I mean . . . what can two women find to talk about for five hours?'

'It's quite easy for them, if I recall Jennifer accurately. Well, here we are, St Swithin's Walk. Been here a few times . . . it's just one of those streets.'

'Aye, every town has many such.'

Number 69, St Swithin's Walk revealed itself to be boldly painted in white with black trim. Hennessey rapped the doorknocker twice, then paused, then rapped it again. The classic 'policeman's knock', tap, tap . . . tap. He had first heard it when still quite young and it held a special resonance for him.

The door was opened slowly. A young girl, about ten, in black spectacles and a pink frock, stood on the threshold blinking at the officers.

Hennessey smiled at her. 'Is your mummy home, pet?'

The small girl nodded. She remained standing still.

'Well, could you go and ask her to come to the door, please?'

The small girl nodded again and continued to remain motionless. Hennessey was about to say 'now' or 'today' or similar, when suddenly the girl turned and darted back into the gloom of the interior of the house.

He glanced to the side of the door and up to the upper floor of the comfortable-looking terraced house and saw that, in contrast to Mrs Pomfret's house, the occupant of this house had opened her windows. 'We'll be able to breathe in there,' he said, 'if we're allowed inside.'

'If,' echoed Yellich.

'We'll be asked in. Nobody wants cops on their doorstep in this street.'

A woman came to the door. She was in her mid-forties, dark-coloured slacks and white cotton blouse, short, dark hair. Hennessey thought she looked worried.

'Yes?' She spoke with a voice that seemed to 'crack' with fear.

'Mrs Silcock?'

'Yes.'

'Police.' Hennessey showed his ID; Yellich did likewise.

'Oh . . .' The woman turned. 'Pamela, go upstairs to your room . . . Now! Never mind why . . . Just . . . go.' She turned to Hennessey and Yellich. 'You'd better come in, don't want to give the neighbours any more to talk about than we have to.'

Hennessey and Yellich stepped up the stone steps and crossed the threshold of the small terraced house, following Mrs Silcock into the cool shade within. Courtesy of open windows, front and back, the air within, by contrast to Emily Pomfret's house, was fresh and breathable.

'So?' Mrs Silcock turned and faced the officers after closing the door to the upstairs, thus doubly ensuring that her daughter was out of earshot. 'What can I do you for?'

'We're actually looking for your husband, Mrs Silcock.'

'I thought as much.' She seemed to be regaining her confidence. 'So, when you find him, tell him his supper's gone cold.'

'His supper?' Hennessey repeated, for it still lacked midday. 'Oh . . . you mean . . . ?'

'Yes, I mean he didn't come home last night. First time

I slept alone without my husband was when he got arrested. I lay there all night, thinking, fearing the worst . . . He's been killed . . . lost his life in an accident, I thought, leaving me alone with Pamela.'

'He didn't phone you?'

'No . . . he used his one phone call to call his brother, asked him to phone me in the morning to tell me where he was. It was his strange way of caring. Won't you sit down?'

The front room of the Silcocks' house was, thought Hennessey, very homely. The door opened directly on to the street, as with all houses in Holgate, yet the Silcocks had still clearly managed to make their front room their 'best' room, in which to entertain guests or sit as a family watching television. The armchairs were deep and had been recently re-covered in a fabric showing red roses on a white background; the bookshelves, which stood against the wall beside the TV, showed a collection of books, and not, as Hennessey had come to expect, a video collection. He sat with gratitude.

'So, what's he done now?' Mrs Silcock allowed a note of resignation to enter her voice.

'We don't know. He may not be involved in anything.'

'Oh, he is. He will have been. He didn't come home last night, which means he's been up to badness. It always does.'

'Do you know a person called Ray Pomfret?'

Mrs Silcock sighed and put her hand to her head. 'That idiot? You know he's been in gaol?'

'Yes.'

'Well, Ian's a good man, he's just very easily led and he never lost his little boy fascination with cars. You'll have read the file?'

'No . . . I . . . we haven't. We came straight here from Emily Pomfret's house.'

'Zombie Emily? I swear if she takes any more pills she'll be walking backwards. That house of hers, you'll have seen it?'

'Yes.'

'Well . . . Ian used to work for a travel agent's, nothing special, but he was on the ladder, managing a small shop, then a bigger one. We got by, but he used to moonlight as a delivery driver, driving cars from a car hire firm or a car dealer in York to wherever they were needed . . . good money . . . got him out on Sundays and whichever weekday he had off, got him all over; Manchester, Newcastle . . . London a few times, got cash in hand and return rail fare. He liked it better than his main job. Didn't have to think, he said, didn't have forms to fill in, didn't have to deal with stupid people who want their money back after their holiday because it rained most of the time – like he was responsible for the weather. Those people, they work themselves up into a rage, then come into the shop mob-handed, screaming and shouting, frightening some customers . . . amusing others.'

'He said that?'

'No . . . well, yes and no. Yes, he said that, but no in the sense he didn't tell me about it, I saw it for myself. That's where we met, in the travel agency . . . everything from a weekend break in Skegness to a Cunard cruise. You name it, we sold it.' She paused. 'Happy days. Trouble was I didn't realize it. High point of my life, a receptionist in a travel agency.' She smiled. 'Some high point. Well, the birth of my daughter, that has to be *the* high point, but me and Ian were going steady, talking about getting married. I read once that marriage is the only feast where the starter is better than the main course . . . how right that is. You married?'

'Widower,' Hennessey said.

'I am,' Yellich replied.

'Well, anyway, one day Ian was asked to ferry a Mercedes-Benz from Southampton to Edinburgh.' She shook her head. 'In hindsight he should have known because the tourist industry works closely with the police, as you know, in the drug war.'

'Yes.'

'Any naïve-looking young man or woman who seems a bit nervous, buys a return ticket to Bangkok with only a two day stopover . . . means only one thing.'

'A courier?'

'Yes. So we inform the police. It's not as obvious as that but there are known drug-smuggling routes and known profiles of drug smugglers . . . young, don't look married, purchase tickets with hard cash . . . that sort of thing, all gets fed to the police.'

'Yes . . . we are grateful, though neither myself nor Sergeant Yellich work in the drug squad, but thanks.'

'Well, should he have known or should he have known, what's Southampton but a port and one of the main points of entry for illegal substances? And what is Edinburgh but the drug capital of Scotland? Worse than Glasgow, they say, but all Ian saw was a dream of a drive in a dream of a car . . . the little boy he is inside. So he took Saturday off, went down to Southampton on the Friday, picked up the vehicle from a man who met him in a car park in Southampton on the Saturday morning . . . that was unusual but he still didn't suspect anything . . . and was told to leave the car parked outside an address in Edinburgh. No paperwork, nothing. Still alarm bells didn't ring, he just wanted to get behind the wheel of a top-of-the-range Merc.'

'So . . . don't tell me . . . it was full of heroin?'

'Cannabis.'

'Heavens, if it had been heroin or coke he was carrying north, he'd still be inside now. But it was blow. He got pulled on the Great North Road, near St Albans. He pleaded

guilty but his brief was able to persuade the judge that he
was an unwitting player in the game, he was of previous
good character and he helped your boys all he could. He
collected four years. He was out in two, just over, but he
was finished, no one would employ him. He met Pomfret
in Full Sutton. Lived just a short walk from here and they
meet for the first time in prison, but Emily, the Zombie,
will have told you that.'

'Yes, she did.'

'Well, that was the end of him, probably should have
started divorce proceedings but then he started going out
and coming back with cash. Not a regular income, a roll
of money, then nothing for a week or two, then another
handful of money, then nothing for a month, and it went
on like that.'

'Do you know where it came from? The money.'

Mrs Silcock remained silent. 'This didn't come from
me, he's my husband. I've got to face him.'

'Understood.'

'I won't sign a statement. I won't give evidence in court.'

'Alright.'

'A man called Hollander.'

'Hollander?' Hennessey glanced at Yellich. 'Do we
know that name?'

'Rings a distant bell,' Yellich replied.

'Does, doesn't it? Hollander ... Hollander ...
Hollander, can't place it.'

'Well, when he came out of gaol, Ian looked lost, then
overnight he changed. Instead of looking aimless and
lethargic, he was like a coiled spring. It was as though
he'd got himself into something that he couldn't get out
of. It was then that the money started to come in. You
know, handfuls of fivers once every so often.'

'Yes. Interesting.'

'Few months ago ... in the winter, we were watching

the news on TV about the floods in York, all those houses along the Ouse by Kings Staith, and there was the sound of a car outside –' she pointed to the open window – 'and Ian stiffened. The car door opened and shut, then someone banged on our door. Not a gentle tap, but a hammering. Ian leapt to his feet and opened the door. I heard a man say, "Mr Hollander wants you," and Ian just grabbed his jacket and went. He said, "I'll be back later," and he did come back with money in his pocket. I don't know who Hollander is . . . or was . . . but what was clear was that whoever he is, or was, he gets or got what he wants or wanted, and when he wants or wanted it.'

It was Saturday, 11.55 hours.

Five

*in which Hennessey receives interesting informa-
tion, an earlier case is revived and later the Yellichs
are at home to the gentle reader.*

SATURDAY, 13.30 HOURS – 23.10 HOURS

As was their usual pattern, Hennessey and Yellich lunched separately that day. Hennessey took luncheon at the Fish Restaurant on Lendal. Yellich, mindful of his budget, ate in the police canteen. They rendezvoused in Hennessey's office.

'Still can't place that name.' Hennessey handed Yellich a mug of tea. 'Been gnawing away at me all lunchtime.' He sat behind his desk.

'Mistake, I'd say, boss.' Yellich accepted the mug of tea and sat on the chair in front of Hennessey's desk. 'Trying to remember something.'

'You mean it'll come of its own accord?'

'Yes, boss, seems to be the case with me. Sitting and trying to remember what you want to remember will not be as effective as getting on with life on a day-to-day basis and then "it", whatever "it" is, will flood into your mind when you are weeding the garden or taking your dog for a walk.'

'Dare say you are right. Certainly trying to remember over lunch hasn't produced a result.' Hennessey settled back in his chair and cradled the hot mug of tea in both hands. 'Anyway . . . this p.m. . . . any thoughts?'

'Seems to have come to a full stop until Pomfret and Silcock turn up. I think they'll have a tale to tell.' He supped his tea. 'But until then . . .'

'Until then we have to force the pace, keep up the momentum. We are still only hours into the investigation, the trail is still hot, we have to be proactive.'

'Yes, sir.'

'Well, I am going for a walk, I can think of a gentleman who might well be most useful. I'd like you to chase up Gary Sledge's associates, his brother mentioned a mate of his.'

'Andy Styles?'

'Yes, and a girl . . . possibly a romantic liaison.'

'Yes . . . what was her name? Heather Lyall . . . yes, that was it, we'll probably get more out of those two than the "Foxy" Stafford, Christopher Kingston crew.'

'See where we get to. See you back here. I'll be finished well before you, so I am pretty well guaranteed to be back first, then, depending what we turn up, we'll decide whether to come in tomorrow or not. We won't if we can avoid it.'

'Yes, boss. Sara would appreciate that.'

Hennessey nodded. 'Yes . . . thanks for coming in today, I appreciate it.' He stood.

Yellich also stood and put the now empty mug on the newspaper-covered table in the corner of Hennessey's office. He glanced out of the window and as he did so, the sky was still vast and blue; the grey walls glinted in the sunlight above the lush grass embankment. Atop the wall were tourists and locals alike, weaving and mingling in brightly coloured clothing. York: high summer.

Hennessey screwed on his Panama, signed out, and crossed the road to Micklegate Bar and followed the walls to Baile Hill, walking en route past the grassed-over terrace where just two days earlier the body of Gary Sledge had been noticed by an astute citizen, who was not the first to observe the prostrate body, but was the first to realize the body spoke not of a nap in the sun, but the longest, the most sinister, the most permanent type of sleep: the long goodbye. Now no longer a crime scene, the terrace was at that moment being enjoyed by two children and their dog who competed for a frisbee. How transitory, Hennessey pondered, as he strolled along, how transitory can sometimes be the nature of tragedy. Life goes on.

He left the walls at Baile Hill and negotiated the summer-swelled traffic at the Tower Street, Skeldergate Bridge junction, turned right on to Tower Street and then left into Piccadilly and glanced at Dick Turpin's grave as he passed the small cemetery on the corner. He entered the area of mixed housing and turned into a small cul-de-sac at the bottom of which was the Gaping Goose.

Hennessey lowered his head as he ingressed the low doorway of 'the Goose' and was relieved to enter the cool of the wood-panelled entrance, with its naked floorboards and the pale cream-painted plaster walls. It was pleasingly quiet in 'the Goose', the pub having escaped the ravages of 'modernization', which, in Hennessey's eyes, had done nothing but reduce many a beautiful and ancient alehouse to the level of an amusement arcade. He turned into the snug, a small room of round tables and a bench running round the walls which at intervals had solid armrests of carved, polished oak. Equally solid chairs stood on the floor at the other side of the tables. Small windows, two on one wall, a third on the other wall, let in natural light, and electric light was provided by a single shaded bulb which hung in the centre of the ceiling. Old, faded prints of nautical scenes were attached to the wall. The bar was in the corner of the room, little more than a serving hatch with a single beer engine in view.

'Mr Hennessey!' The man sat in the corner of the room furthest from both the door and the bar, the one seat where all the room could be surveyed.

'"Shored-up" –' Hennessey smiled – 'I thought I might find you here.'

'Well, here or one or two other hostelries for the discerning patron, Mr Hennessey.'

'Quiet, out of the way, just the place for someone who doesn't want to be seen too often, by too many. Dangerous life you lead, Shored-up.'

'A double whisky, Bells with ice, please.' The man smiled. 'Just to save you asking.'

Hennessey bought the drink plus a soda water and lime for himself from the quiet and emotionally distant barman and carried them over to where 'Shored-up' sat. 'So three weeks out, how's life treating you?'

'You consulted my file, Mr Hennessey.'

'Yes.' He sat in a chair opposite the man. 'Had to make sure you were out and about. Would have been easier if you had been on the inside, just a quick drive and a chat in the agent's room.'

'Ugh . . .' Shored-up shuddered, 'those awful prison shirts and but one bath a week. You even have to share a cell and share other things as well, the shame, the degradation.' The man was short, finely built, wearing an expensive-looking, lightweight, Italian-styled jacket and an equally expensive-looking shirt and a yellow chequered cravat.

'Still hitting the charity shops I see, Shored-up?' Hennessey sipped his drink.

'Mr Hennessey –' Shored-up looked disappointed – 'cynicism doesn't become you.'

'Let's just call it an eye for detail. Look how frayed your cuffs are, and pink buttons on a green jacket . . . come on.'

'Ah . . .' Shored-up examined the cuffs of his jacket and

then glanced at the buttons. 'I confess I hadn't noticed either but you must agree, the cut is exquisite. All for three pounds in a charity shop . . .'

'Three quid?'

'All . . .' He held up a Panama hat which had lain beside him on the leather-covered bench. 'Hat and jacket for three pounds. Not bad. Helps cut the dash. Very important in my line of work.'

'Your line of work. The sort that gets you six months in prison. What happened there? Your record said "fraud", – that covers a multitude of wrongdoings.'

'Doesn't it just?' Shored-up lifted the whisky to his lips, savoured the aroma and then sipped delicately. 'Going inside is good for the soul, it makes you appreciate the finer things in life. I have pondered raising enough capital to open a private prison . . . I consider myself particularly well qualified for the task . . . each inmate would have his own cell and alcohol with each cooked meal.'

Hennessey put his hand to his head. 'You've seriously lost the plot now.'

'I bought a car with a cheque.'

'Which bounced?'

'But of course. That was the whole point of the story. Wouldn't have worked if the cheque had cleared. Lonely lady, so full of charm . . . so eager to help a disadvantage gentleman like myself.'

'Well, disadvantaged . . . that bit I would go along with.'

'She had a number of cars left to her by her late husband, she only drove one small one . . . and three larger ones, two of which she had wanted to keep for sentimental reasons, but the third she didn't care for . . . it was large and had bad associations for her.'

'Large?'

Shored-up held his palms vertically. 'About . . . about Rolls-Royce size. Except that it was a Bentley.'

'Ah.'

'So . . . well, after a few weeks of afternoon teas followed by bridge in the conservatory, I began to tell her about our family business.'

'Yes . . .' Hennessey nodded, 'a goldmine in South Africa.'

'Tin in Bolivia . . .'

'Yes . . . of course, and you being a Major in the Green Howards, retired . . .'

'Devon and Dorsets. I think I told you last time we met. Too much danger of running into the real thing up here, so I changed my allegiance to a regiment of the southern counties.'

'Probably sensible . . . from your point of view, I mean.'

'Well, this lady was a little shrewd, shrewder than I thought.'

'Poor you.'

'Yes, indeed. She didn't offer to lend me a little money to tide the business over though her income wasn't unlike the Gross National Product of Bolivia itself . . . I caught sight of the bank statement.'

'I bet you did. Very early on in your association if I know you, Shored-up.'

'That's just good business, Mr Hennessey. A man like me, in my line of work has to be sure of his mark.'

'I'll say.'

'Anyway, she did offer to sell me the Bentley for a low but reasonable price. She'd get some money and more importantly she'd clear a bit of space in her garage which is what she seemed to want more than anything. I would have the car attended to – upgraded, sell it for a profit and make a little money for myself. So I agreed . . . of course.'

'Of course.'

'Delayed a little because a public holiday was in the

offing, that would increase the ten working days my cheque would take to clear to sixteen actual days, by which time I had hoped to sell the vehicle on.'

'So by the time milady was in possession of a bouncing cheque, you would be long gone?'

'Not long gone. I planned to associate with her as her lunch and afternoon companion until the day before my cheque would be returned to her with a massive black stamp across the face of it, by which time I would have sold the Bentley . . . hopefully for cash or a building society cheque.'

'And . . .'

'Well, no buyers, but all was not lost because I still had the Bentley safe in a lock-up. By then I was the registered owner, in my real name of course.'

'Oh, but of course.'

'But my friend knew me only as Lt Colonel Smythe.'

'Smith? Not very original.'

'With a "y" and an "e".'

Hennessey nodded. 'That's more like you.'

'But pronounced "Smith", less pompous than "Smythe", which my companion appreciated. You have to know how to play your targets in my game. Whatever may be their own particular proclivities, you must play to them.'

'So how was it you were nicked? You could have got away with that one.'

'Well, as I said, milady was shrewder than most . . . she kept a little insurance, no wonder she was happy to let the car go.'

'What was that? A hidden camera?'

'Nothing so high-tech. Just my dabs.' Shored-up wiggled his fingertips in the air. 'My fickle friends. I should have them surgically removed, such is possible, I hear.'

'Such is.'

'Anyway, to tell the story. After we had met for lunch

a few times I realized I had a "biter". I was invited back to her house, and by house, I mean house . . . out in the Vale, a garden like Hyde Park and that's just the front.'

'I get the picture.'

'Anyway she showed me round the ground floor . . . never got upstairs.'

'Bad luck.'

'Showed me this and that and was very keen to show me her silver collection; unlocked the display cabinet and let me handle pretty well every piece. Then we went to the conservatory and sat in the afternoon sun playing cards. All very civilized.'

'Very trusting of her.'

'Well, I am not a violent man and she had a servant in the house, and a gardener outside.' Shored-up paused and sipped his whisky. 'Nectar of the Gods,' he voiced with relish. 'Well, came the day the cheque bounced and I didn't turn up for our lunch date and milady put two and two together, realized she'd been had, called the police and must have said, "I only know him as Lt Col. Smythe, retired, but should he be known to you, his fingerprints are all over my silverware collection." So it was that she was reunited with her Bentley and I was reunited with Her Majesty's Prison Service: felons for the disposal of. Six months, and that's with remission. I always get remission . . . a model prisoner.'

'You ingratiate yourself everywhere you go. You know, trying to get hold of your personality is like trying to nail jelly to a wall.'

Shored-up smiled. 'But you didn't seek me on this fine summer's day to enquire after my health and welfare?'

'No . . . no, I didn't.' Hennessey drained his glass. Shored-up did likewise. 'Same again, thanks.'

'Not so fast. You'll either earn your next drink or you'll buy it yourself.'

'Mr Hennessey . . .' said with a feigned protest.

'Depends how you help me, Shored-up.'

'You know, Mr Hennessey . . .' he, with what Hennessey thought a more than forlorn hope, pushed his empty glass towards Hennessey, 'always ready to help the police.'

'Complete the sentence, Shored-up –' Hennessey couldn't resist a smile – 'remember what I said just now about your personality, a nail, a wall and a lump of jelly? You are always ready to help the police once you're caught bang to rights, no room for manoeuvre, collared in a vice-like grip and then, and only then, are you willing to co-operate. Up to that point you slither like a fish out of water.'

'You do me an injustice, Mr Hennessey.' But at least this time he didn't push his empty glass in Hennessey's direction.

'That's the big problem with people like you, Shored-up, you believe your own fantasies. 'So what do you know about a man, possibly a felon called Hollander?'

'Dutchy!'

Hennessey's hand went up to his forehead. 'Dutchy! Dutchy Hollander . . . of course . . . of course. Me and my sergeant knew we'd heard that name somewhere. If only the guy had said "Dutchy" we would have twigged straight away. We're just so unused to hearing him called by his proper name . . . that and not hearing about him for some time.'

'So, why the interest?'

'That's for us to know.'

'If you want my help, Mr Hennessey.'

'If you don't want me to bounce you inside on any one of all those warrants under your aliases, which you have accumulated, you'll leave it at that. It's for us to know.'

'Ah . . . speaking of a warrant, I haven't been to see my probation officer.'

'You were sentenced to prison, plus a period of probation?'

'Well . . . yes . . .'

'And how often have you seen your PO?'

'Not very often.'

'How often?'

'I haven't, actually.'

'Not once!'

'No . . . actually. I'm sure he's a very nice gentleman, or a very nice lady, but POs are like doctors, they look so young these days. I don't mind listening to a doctor who is still fresh because there I listen to learned knowledge.'

'Well, that's a sliver of humility that I never thought I'd see in you, Shored-up.'

The man smiled. 'But being told how to conduct myself by a twenty-year-old, with no life experience, that I find difficult. So, I was wondering if you could perhaps persuade the powers that be that I really am of greater use outwith the confines of prison than within?'

'Use to who?'

'Well . . . both of us really.'

'I'd go and see your PO as soon as I could if I were you. So . . . tell me about Dutchy Hollander.'

'The biggest crook without a criminal record, Mr Hennessey. A dram would help me remember.'

'A glass of orange juice would help you remember much better.'

'Oh, that would ruin my palate.'

'So, talk to me.'

'Well, you don't know him . . . you know of him, but know him . . . no way. He pays others to do his dirty work. He's just a person you don't want to know. Made his money in property. His trick was to buy tenanted properties, old houses with tenants in them so he becomes the landlord, that way he gets the property for half what it would be worth if it was vacant property. Then he does what any self-respecting landlord would do, drives out his tenants, makes their lives hell, doesn't actually evict them and gets into a legal battle . . . No . . . first he doubles the rent, then he cuts off the heating, then the electricity supply. If that doesn't work, he vandalizes the cars, or has them vandalized . . . by which time only the diehard tenants are left, thinking that the law is on their side, which it is, but only on paper. It's then that Dutchy Hollander sends in the "visitors".'

'The visitors?'

'That's what he calls them. They're his persuaders, very good at approaching, wearing ski masks . . . in the gloom of the property, just inside the front door, waiting for them when they come home from work. Point out to them in terms certain that they are messing with the most dangerous man in the Vale of York, and being right in the eyes of the law is no help in a dark place where there are no witnesses. "Fancy waking up in hospital with your head and both arms and legs in plaster?" they say. That's followed up by a "Get out" and that is followed up by a punch in the stomach, and being female won't save you. If that doesn't work, and it usually does, try coming home to a flat full of dead cats. I mean dead cats everywhere, cats not just on the floor of your flat, but in the toilet bowl, in the shower, or both, in your bed, in the drawers of your dressing table. The sensible ones get out quickly. It's healthier, I mean for them. They have a sense that they're leaving because they want to. The ones that stick to their rights and principles leave eventually, they all do, but they depart with a sense that they are leaving because they have to, a feeling of being forced out, leaving on Dutchy Hollander's terms and that stays with them for the rest of their life. As they say, "Pride is pride and pain is pain . . . but failure lasts a lifetime." So the clever ones swallow their pride and ease their pain and go without a fuss, they're only renting after all. It's a stepping-stone to a mortgage, anyway. The ones that dig their heels in are the ones who get grief and where is the man during this?'

'Where?'

'Nowhere to be seen, that's where. Or with a cast-iron alibi . . . on a waterskiing and diving holiday in the Seychelles . . . it'll all be done verbally. He'll contract it out, a chat in a car or somewhere where it can't be overheard. He'll say. "This is the address . . . big old house, got fifteen tenants, all young professionals . . . you've got two months to clear it, anyway you like, just don't let anything lead back to me. The sooner you get the job done, the bigger the drink, but two months tops." So he gets his hands on the house, which he then sells as "vacant possession", doubled his money in two months, less the cost of his "visitors". He's done that a few times in the last ten years.'

'Pleasant character.'

'You'll know of him, I think, but in terms of your records, your computer database, he's as white as the driven snow.'

'And you know that this is how he works . . . we've only heard his name.'

'No. I know that is how he is *rumoured* to work.'

'Good enough.'

'I make my time inside work for me, Mr Hennessey.'

'Has he offed anyone?'

'There are such rumours, but not any of his tenants, he stops short of murdering them to get them to hand their keys back, but he's a man with fingers in many pies and, yes, he is rumoured to have offed a few. Or at least had them offed.'

'A few?'

'Yes, over the years. He's got a hit man called "Frost-bite", so I hear tell.'

'Frostbite?'

'So they say is his name.'

'Where does Hollander live?'

For that information Shored-up was able to negotiate another double Bells.

'So –' Hennessey sat down, having purchased another soft drink for himself – 'what's the answer? Where does he live?'

'Out by Stamford Bridge.'

'Conveniently close to Full Sutton, where he ought to be residing by the sound of it.'

'As you say, Mr Hennessey.' Shored-up raised his glass in a gesture of 'good health' and also of thanks. 'In a village called Kempley Bridge. Can't miss his house, yellow-painted monster.'

'Yellow!'

'So they say, all woodwork, doors, window frames, the fence surrounding the property, the double doors of the garage, all yellow. He wasn't particularly welcome in the village. The local squire, in his plus fours, called on him one day, ranting about his yellow house scaring the game and spoiling the shooting. The publican of the Merrie Monk, being the only watering hole in the village, refused to serve him. I mean, didn't say he wasn't being served, just ignored him, left Dutchy Hollander standing there like a spare part while he served others that had come in after him. That didn't go down too well with Dutchy, so they say.'

'So, what happened?'

'Made use of his "visitors", didn't he? Don't know what they said to the squire in his plus fours but he never both-ered Dutchy again, and the publican of the Merrie Monk, well, he wasn't there to open up the pub one day and the day after he was learning how to pull pints with one of his arms in a cast. After that he would jump to serve Dutchy whenever Dutchy came in for a beer or two, especially if he had friends with him.'

'Sounds like a man we should get to know better.'

'Well, he's one of the clever ones. I mean the really clever ones. Never even seen the inside of a police station let alone a prison. Doesn't let anybody near him, contracts out his jobs. Always has an alibi for anything that goes down that might be connected to him.'

Hennessey smiled. 'Confess I rather like alibi merchants, they're brittle . . . if you can destroy the alibi . . . You mention the clever ones. Believe me, Shored-up, the really clever ones don't provide an alibi. That's clever.'

'I'll remember that.'

'Well, given the way you leave your dabs everywhere, you'll need more than that to keep you out of the slammer.'

'Yes –' Shored-up cast a glance sideways – 'I was somewhat outwitted there. Who would have thought it, a frail, elderly lady? She thought ahead, covered her bases, and anticipated every eventuality. Who would have thought it?'

'Who indeed?'

'Well, win some, lose some. I'll put it down to experience. I probably wouldn't have fallen for it if she had asked me to look at some old photographs, but her silverware, I couldn't resist touching that. That's one to chalk up to experience.' He forced a smile. 'A man of my experience too.'

'So, you're just out of the pokey, your ear's to the ground as usual?'

'But discreetly so, Mr Hennessey. I ask you to appreciate that. Were I to be seen in conversation with you, like this is a pub, well certain circles would become closed to me. It is in both our interests to be discreet.'

'Of course.' Hennessey leaned forward. 'Saturday today . . . on Wednesday afternoon a body was found just inside the walls, a known felon by the name of Sledge. One of the Sledges of Tang Hall.'

'Yes, I read of it and also saw the local television news. So is this the reason for your warm and pleasant company?'

'Yes, in a word.' Hennessey found his own voice had dropped to a whisper, though for no logical reason. He allowed it to remain at a whisper; he felt it added a sense of urgency. 'He was drilled, a small calibre bullet. Went in here . . .' he put his finger to his head behind his left ear, 'and it stayed in . . . no exit wound.'

'Nasty.'

'Well, also neat, efficient. The bullet spun round and round the grey stuff looking for a way out.'

'Sort of . . .'

'Sort of gangland, I'd say. So, what do you know? What have you heard?'

'Nothing. Scout's honour.'

'But you know in which direction to incline your ear.'

'Perhaps.'

'So, incline. I'll see what I can do for you when you're lifted for not going to see your PO and I'll see what I can do about keeping your aliases to myself for the time being and so long as they pertain only to petty offences.'

'Oh, passing petty, I assure you, Mr Hennessey, passing petty, of minor import, mere blemishes on the fabric of our society.'

'Well . . . we'll see.' Suddenly Hennessey was, in his mind, thirty years younger, placating a demanding son with, 'We'll see.' He brought himself back to the here and now. 'Two more names, both ex-cons, white collars, both of this town . . . Silcock and Pomfret. Names mean anything? Ian and Raymond.'

'Isn't Pomfret a mate of "Big Ben"?'

Hennessey shrugged. 'Dunno, I give in. Is he a mate of "Big Ben"?'

'Not many Pomfrets in the Vale or the city, it's not a common name, fewer still will be villains . . . Raymond Pomfret?'

'He's got a drum in Holgate. His name was mentioned in connection with Dutchy Hollander. Sounds like he was one of Hollander's men, his wife gave us that impression.'

'What does he say?'

'We've yet to talk to him, him and Silcock. Thought that you might know something whilst I am picking your brains.'

'I'll . . . I'll ask about . . . ask around.'

'If you would.' Hennessey stood. 'You know where I can be contacted.'

'There'll be something in it for me?'

'Yes. In direct proportion to the value of what you provide for me. You come up with the goods, then I'll come up with the goods.'

Yellich turned off Bad Bargain Lane and into Rydal Avenue and allowed the car to coast to a halt. It was as he had predicted: if you don't try to remember something, it will push itself to the forefront of your mind soon enough. Hollander, 'Dutchy' Hollander, that name had often been in the background whenever something serious has gone down. Like the devil himself, often mentioned, often blamed, but never seen. Despite the heat, Yellich felt a chill creep up his spine, and when was he last mentioned?' Recently . . . months ago . . . then he spoke aloud. 'Jane Seymour,' he said. 'Of course.' He reached for the radio in the car and pressed the send button. 'DS Yellich.'

'Yes, sir,' the response crackled.

'C.R., please.'

'Criminal Records,' the voice similarly crackled.

'DS Yellich. Can you find me anything you've got on one "Dutchy" Hollander. Yes, Hollander is his surname,

"Dutchy" is his nickname. He's in his early sixties, lives out east of York, near Stamford Bridge. I have visited him. Cross-refer it to the Jane Seymour murder case, that's dated last year. Thanks. Out.' He replaced the microphone. He stared at the narrow canyon that was Rydal Avenue, aware and unconcerned about people looking at him with more than minimal curiosity. The murder of Gary Sledge, the murder of Jane Seymour, and Hollander's name is there in the background in both cases. This investigation now, he thought, now takes on a new meaning. He drove on and parked outside number 37, left and locked his car and knocked on the door of the home of Andy Styles.

He was greeted with cold-eyed hostility from Styles, which evaporated the moment Styles realized that Yellich was not investigating him, but seeking information in respect of the murder of Gary Sledge, upon which Styles displayed a warm 'Anything I can do to help' attitude.

Yellich was invited into the living room of the Styleses' house. Yellich found it a pleasant, cleanly kept home – carpet on the floor, solid furniture, horse brasses hanging on the wall, expensive-looking television and a hi-fi in the corner, shelves which contained a mixture of books and videos, with a tendency, he noted, more towards the latter. It was neat – everything in its place – with a smell of air freshener and, beneath that, the gentle odour of wood polish. The windows were open and the lace curtains wafted in the occasional breeze. Styles was a muscular youth, dressed in a white T-shirt which said 'Benidorm' on the front, and faded, torn denims. He was barefoot, had a surprising absence of tattoos and wore no decoration. He wore his hair short but neatly cut. He could, thought Yellich, have worn a suit without difficulty. He invited Yellich to sit down, as he fell back on to a settee, curled one leg up underneath him, which Yellich thought to be an unusually 'laid back' and 'hippie'-like posture for a Tang Hall 'hard man'.

'Yeah, Gary.' He had a soft Yorkshire accent. 'Bad news that. My parents are out, otherwise we'd have to go and sit in your car or go to the police station ... they don't like the Sledges, don't like me ... didn't like me mixing with Gary. I'm the only one in this house who's been in trouble with the law and they think that's because I mixed with Gary Sledge. They're probably right. Mind you, I'm glad I'm seen as a mate of Gary's right now, you've no idea what it's like on this estate right now ... the Sledges are out for blood. I've been left alone because I was his best mate and Gary's brother, Shane ... he's in Armley.'

'I know. I visited him.'

'Well, he put in a word for me ... but things have been a bit ... a bit ... ready to erupt.'

'Tense?'

'Aye ... that's the word. Like ready to snap. Some people have been leaned on but the main suspects are all inside; Kingston, Burton, Diamond, Phil Corr ... the Sledges just know they had something to do with it but can't get at them. They rolled Ernie Diamond's brother last night but he didn't cough to anything. Corr's brother was seen running off the estate carrying a suitcase, no idea where he's gone but one day Kingston and his crew will be on the outside and the Sledges will be waiting ... ten years, fifteen, s'OK ... the Sledges won't forget.'

Yellich's small house in Huntingdon suddenly seemed very warm and very inviting. Life on the housing estates was clearly different. People don't live on estates like Tang Hall, he thought, they survive. 'Well, the reason I'm here, Andy ... the reason I'm here, is because Shane Sledge suggested it.'

'Shane said that?'

'Yes.'

'Not like one of the Sledges to do that, even if the police are trying to find out who murdered one of theirs.'

'Well, like I said, I visited Shane and he didn't strike me as being a very Sledge-like Sledge, if you see what I mean.'

'Yes . . . aye . . . Shane, he's a bit soft, he's not made for the street. If Shane Sledge is going to be a crim he's going to be a white-collar crim . . . fraud, embezzlement . . . that's Sean's style and, even then, he won't be right comfortable with it. Basically I don't think Shane's got it in him at all.'

'And what about you?'

'Me? I don't like being known to the police, I don't like my prints being on file . . . but, no qualifications, I can turn a window, slide into someone's house, slide out again a few minutes later and make more than I could earn for two weeks hard graft on a building site. You see the attraction of crime?'

'I do.' Yellich nodded. 'I don't agree with it, but for an unemployed and possibly unemployable young man or woman, yes, I can understand the temptation . . . never seen it lead anywhere I'd want to go and, as in the reason for my visit, I've seen it lead to a bullet in the head and that's somebody still in their early twenties. Liberty, life itself, that has a value that many young criminals ignore but yes, I can quite understand the attraction, short-term and superficial as it is, I can understand it.' He paused. 'Anyway, if you want to help your mate, you'll help me.'

'OK.' Styles looked uncomfortable. 'I'm not going to testify. I won't sign a statement. Anything I say is off the record.'

'Alright, for the time being.'

'For the time being? I mean never.'

'Well, if you have vital information, you could be forced to testify, but we'll see where we get. Now, you know that Gary Sledge's drum was turned over?'

'Yes, that's the rumour.'

'Well, it's more than rumour, somebody was looking for something. They took away a pile of folding green but that was . . . that was plunder. They were searching for something and we believe that what they were searching for is the key to this investigation. So what was it? Would Heather Lyall know?'

Styles shot a glance at Yellich.

'We know about her.' Yellich spoke softly. 'We've yet to meet her but we know about her.' He paused then he threw in a wild card. 'We also know about Pomfret, Silcock and Dutchy Hollander.'

Styles gasped. 'So what do you need me for?'

'To help us glue the pieces together. We're particularly interested in Hollander.'

'I bet you are.' Styles sat back. 'You want to talk about Hollander to the Sledges.'

'Oh?'

'Yes, they . . . they "visit" people for Dutchy Hollander.'

'Really! They're his minders?'

'Among others.'

Yellich thought, Wheels within wheels, but said, 'So what were they looking for?'

'Who?'

'Kingston and crew. They were searching for something when they turned over Gary Sledge's flat. So, like I have already asked, what was it?'

Styles put his hand to his head. 'I told him not to do it, but he was a Sledge, thought he was untouchable, thought he was safe, even from Dutchy Hollander.'

Yellich fell silent. He thought for a moment and then asked, 'Did Gary Sledge have something on Hollander?'

Styles nodded. 'He was putting the squeeze on him.'

'What was it?'

Styles shook his head. 'Whatever it was, it was something that could put Hollander away for a very long time.

Heather Lyall might help you. I've said all I'm going to say and between you and me, that's nothing. Understand? Folk round here will see the plod have called, I'll say I was questioned about a break-in.'

'Alright.' Yellich stood. 'This is good. I'll say the same. That's how it works, you help us, we help you. So you don't know anything about the break-in at that chemist's last night?'

'No.' Styles smiled his thanks.

'And your parents will alibi you?'

'Yes, I was here all evening.'

'Well, no more to be said. I'll see myself out. Thanks for your time.'

Yellich, pleased with himself, tapped on the frame of the doorway of Hennessey's office. 'I know who Hollander is.' He brandished the file that C.R. had obtained for him on the murder of Jane Seymour.

'So do I.' Hennessey beamed back. 'Come and tell me what you know.'

Yellich sat in front of Hennessey's desk and told him of his visit to Andrew Styles. In return, Hennessey told Yellich of his meeting with Shored-up. They then examined the file.

'So,' Hennessey said, 'my snout was right and he was wrong. We don't know Hollander in the sense that he has a record but wrong in the sense that Hollander has been inside a police station. Prime suspect in the murder of Jane Seymour . . . interviewed at home and here.'

'By me. If Mrs Silcock had said "Dutchy", I would have twigged instantly.'

'Me too.'

'But, "Mr Hollander", that just rang bells.'

'Again, with me too!'

'He had an alibi for her murder and also claiming not

to have known her, signed a statement to that effect, it's in the file.'

'So I see.' Hennessey read the statement. 'Short and brief. Helps us in a sense, no let-out clause . . . you know . . . Sledge had evidence that could destroy Hollander's alibi or he had evidence which proves Hollander knew of Jane Seymour.'

'Or both,' Yellich offered. 'Or both.'

'Indeed. Shored-up said he was an alibi merchant, has grown to depend on them, and his alibi was that he was playing cards at home with—'

Yellich smiled. 'Yes, I read the file before I came here . . . Silcock and Pomfret.'

'And the motive being that Jane was alleging a serious offence against him, it says here.'

'Indecent assault and false imprisonment.'

'Her allegation was investigated.' Hennessey leafed through the file. 'No charges were brought when the Crown witness disappeared.'

'Disappeared?' Hennessey's jaw sagged. 'Just how big is the body count here?'

'Just one. Jane was found battered to death a few weeks later. Other people in the saga remain "missing".'

'What connected her murder to Hollander?'

'Death threats from him for causing him grief,' Yellich replied. 'It's all coming back to me now.'

'Yes, I remember it too. Couldn't break his alibi, no other suspect, so it became a "sticker".' Hennessey glanced at his watch. 'Well, four p.m., neither of us should be here at all. So what do you say we rescue what we can of our weekend and pick this up on Monday? Come back refreshed and "unstick" it?'

'I'd appreciate it, sir.'

'I think I would too.'

*　　　*　　　*

Yellich drove home to his modest new-build house in Huntingdon. He parked his car at the kerb in front of his house and, when walking up the short driveway, was met by Jeremy, who bounded out of the house and impacted with Yellich with such force that Yellich had to brace himself against the collision. He walked into the house and received a second embrace, this time from Mrs Sara Yellich. Yellich peeled off his jacket and asked Sara how her day had been.

'Not bad.' She took his jacket. 'One of our better days.' She smiled at Jeremy, who stood with his parents, beaming with pride. 'He's been a good boy all day. Helped me with the baking and our meal.'

Yellich ran his fingers through Jeremy's hair. 'Good boy.' He smiled. 'So shall we go for a walk?'

Jeremy nodded enthusiastically. Yellich was pleased. It was just as the child psychologist had said it would be: Jeremy was beginning to associate good behaviour with reward. He was beginning to develop foresight. It was a significant milestone in Jeremy's development, and very encouraging. Yellich changed into his jeans and trainers and took Jeremy for a walk across the fields adjacent to the Huntingdon housing estate, to a small wood, identifying trees and plants and birds as they walked. It was a special time for them, a 'quality' time where a father and son bonded. The hour's walk with Daddy was his reward for being a good boy. It was, Yellich had conceded, not at all an imposition: the hour with his son was a source of great joy. Yellich recalled the dismay that he and Sara had felt when told by a grimfaced young paediatrician that their son would not be 'normal'. The fear that hovers over all soon-to-be parents had, for them, been realized. Their dismay was, however, soon replaced with pleasure and interest. Jeremy had grown to prove himself a very giving child despite his handicap and had never lost that childish sense of wonder that evaporates with the onset of teen years. It had also been as if a whole hitherto unknown world had opened up for them as they met other parents of children with 'learning difficulties' and those dedicated professionals who devoted their working life, often with little pay, to the welfare of such children. With care, love and stimulation, they were told, by the time Jeremy was an adult he should have achieved the mental age of twelve years and be capable of semi-independent living in a hostel.

Later that evening, Somerled and Sara Yellich sat in each other's arms on the settee, sharing a bottle of wine and listening to the Promenade Concert broadcast on Radio 3.

'So this is marriage,' Sara intertwined her fingers with those of her husband, '– every little girl's dream.'

'Sorry, it doesn't measure up to fantasy.'

'To think there I was, Miss Medway, teacher of English at a large comprehensive school, I'd be head of department by now, and I let myself get dragged away by the hair . . .'

'Not much hair as I recall. I thought you were male when I first saw you – that short hair, waiflike figure . . . Quite nice though . . .'

'Well, thank you . . .'

'. . . and I don't recall much struggling, you seemed to be very keen to leave teaching.'

Sara curled deeper into Yellich's embrace. 'Yes, it was getting stupidly top-heavy with administration. Gone are the days when teachers only had lessons to prepare and end of term reports to write. Now there are development plans for each pupil, quarterly assessments of staff . . . too many very good teachers are voting with their feet. Glad I'm out of it . . . glad to be here anyway.'

Yellich squeezed her gently.

'Very glad,' she said, 'very, very, very glad.'

Six

in which Yellich meets one of life's survivors

MONDAY, 08.30 – 12.30 HOURS

'I didn't realize how tired I was.' George Hennessey sipped his mug of tea. 'Seemed to catch up with me last night . . . felt very tired at only nine p.m. So I went up, head hit the pillow at nine thirty about, next thing I know it was seven a.m. Felt so refreshed, such a solid night's sleep but ten and a half hours . . . that's a little embarrassing.'

'Like you said, you needed it, boss. It catches up with you.' Yellich too sipped his mug of tea. It was a habit he had picked up from Hennessey and by now, like Hennessey, he felt the mug of tea was necessary to start the day. 'It was a long week.'

'So –' Hennessey turned away from the window of his cramped office and sat at his desk – 'still more questions than answers.'

'Seems so, boss, but we're getting there.'

'You think?' Hennessey smiled.

'Well, we left it focusing on Dutchy Hollander. He's come to sound like a felon I would like to nail. I remember him now, smiling, brimming with confidence, a thin veneer of charm that concealed a vicious personality. It came back yesterday when I was out with Jeremy, he—'

Hennessey's phone rang.

'Excuse me.' Hennessey picked up the phone and Yellich saw Hennessey's eyebrows furrow as he listened. Hennessey said, 'Thank you, I appreciate it.' He put the phone down and held eye contact with Yellich. 'Well, that's a turn-up for the books. It's a turn-up that I didn't expect and a turn-up I like not the sound of.'

'Oh?'

'Yes, well something happened between the Pomfret and the Silcock households over the weekend. One lady clearly went to the door of the other lady . . . I know not with what intention . . . but both came to the police station on Saturday night, just after we had left, by the sound of it . . . That was the collator, by the way.' Hennessey patted the phone with his meaty, fleshy hand, which Yellich noted had more than a few liver spots. 'They wanted to report their husbands as mis pers.'

'Oh . . .'

'Yes, that's what I thought. Anyway, a note was taken but they were told to come back and report them officially when they had been missing for twenty-four hours, as is the procedure in the case of missing adults.'

'Yes.'

'Came back yesterday at fifteen thirty hours and a missing person's file was opened in the case of Raymond Pomfret and Ian Silcock.'

'Well . . . well, that bodes no good.'

'Yes. Collator saw that we had recorded our interest – the computer logs all queries. He phoned to see if I am interested in that development, which of course we are, and as you say, it bodes not well for Silcock and Pomfret.'

'Might loosen a few tongues though. I mean, don't want to count chickens but if ill has befallen those two, then Christopher Kingston and crew might be more willing to talk to us.'

'They might indeed but, like you say, don't want to count chickens . . . so . . . any urge to do anything?'

'In respect of the investigation, you mean?' Yellich grinned.

'Well, yes.' Hennessey laughed. 'Any other urges you'll have to contain.'

'I'd like to go and see Heather Lyall.' Yellich stood.

'Gary Sledge's girlfriend?'

'Yes, skipper.' Yellich drained his mug of tea. 'Shane Styles gave the impression that she might well be a profitable source of inquiry.'

'Very well, you crack on with that. I think I'll familiarize myself with the Jane Seymour murder. It may or may not be relevant. I'd like to be forearmed if it is. Shored-up will take a day or two to come back. Dutchy Hollander isn't going anywhere and he doesn't know of our recent interest in him. We'll leave the Kingston crew on a slow simmer in prison. They'll be ready to talk soon, especially if Pomfret and Silcock are out of the way.'

The eyes, he thought, were the most appealing. They had an honest, innocent, sincere, still a little unworldly, look but not so much as to be able to say naïve. The smile too, that he also found appealing, slightly parted lips showing perfect teeth, the complexion was slightly freckled and the long dark hair was swept back and tied in a ribbon. It was the last photograph taken of Jane Seymour. Hennessey put the photograph back in the file and read the recording. Jane's body had been found on waste ground, having been dumped, it seemed, from a vehicle. Car tyre tracks but no footprints were close to the vehicle. She had been strangled. There were no defensive wounds on the body or traces of her attacker's skin or blood beneath her fingernails. Dr Louise D'Acre, he saw, with more than a little interest, had performed the post-mortem and had found nothing to explain why there should be no defence injuries or traces of her attacker's blood or flesh beneath her fingernails. There had been, for example, no trace of sedative in the bloodstream, no ligature marks on her wrists, which, respectively, would have suggested she had been drugged or restrained. There had been no other injuries. Her stomach had contained a partially digested meal, showing that she had been murdered just hours after she had eaten. Her end had been very sudden and unexpected.

At the time of her death, Jane had been a student at the University of York. She had been between her second and third, final, year but had chosen to remain in York rather than return home, though home was nearby Hutton Cranswick, in the Wolds – less than an hour by train, Hennessey guessed, changing at Driffield. That, he thought, was quite interesting: not a girl to wander far from home when it came to going to university and that sort of girl is unlikely to move in the same circles as a man like Dutchy Hollander, so far as Hennessey's impression of Hollander was beginning to develop. He turned to read her complaint. It was, he found, very brief.

Jane had been working in a bar in York. She had accepted an invitation from other women in the bar to go to an after-work party. She had found herself in Dutchy Hollander's large house and the 'party' Hollander had envisaged had been more in the manner of an orgy. Jane had refused to participate and had wanted to leave and go home. Hollander, she alleged, had grabbed her by the hair, slapped her and pushed her up the stairs of his home to an upstairs room where he had performed a series of indecent assaults. She had successfully resisted rape. Hollander had punched her and locked her in the room, 'until you see sense'. In the night she had opened the window and shinned down a drainpipe and made her way back to York.

There was one partial witness, one David Tebb, who had signed a statement to the effect that he had seen Hollander slap Jane Seymour and push her up the stairs whilst also holding her against her will. Shortly after Hollander was interviewed, Jane Seymour was dead and David Tebb was a 'missing person'. Hennessey closed the file. 'And,' he said aloud, 'he can claim an alibi for that! A party.' Then he thought: Either Jane Seymour's complaint is a tissue of lies or that is one very breakable alibi. He then read the alibi itself. Hollander's statement was short and to the point. He had been at home alone on the evening in question and he did not know nor had ever met Jane Seymour. Yellich's recording stated that Hollander had been shown a photograph of Jane and repeated that he had never met her, nor did he know her by any other name. He glanced at his watch: 09.40. He thought that he would see if he was correct, York to Hutton Cranswick, one hour by rail, change at Driffield.

The house on Long Ridge Lane, Nether Poppleton, was detached. One car stood in the driveway in front of the closed, black-painted doors of the garage. An oil stain behind the car indicated to Yellich that the driveway usually accommodated two cars. He walked up to the front door and pressed the bell. It rang continuously as he pressed it and stopped ringing when he released the pressure. It was clearly linked to the mains electricity circuit of the house, as many doorbells are, though they were not to his taste. He preferred the independent battery-powered bells. Less to go wrong, he thought, and the less there is to go wrong, the less that will go wrong. The door was opened by a slender young woman in jeans, flip-flop sandals and a green T-shirt. She blushed when she saw Yellich. 'Police?'

Yellich nodded. ''Fraid so.' He remained stone-faced.

'You come to arrest me?' she hissed.

107

'No. Are you Heather Lyall?'

'Yes,' she hissed. 'Keep your voice down, will you?' She stepped out over the doorframe, half closing the door behind her.

'Who is it, dear?' The piercing voice came from within the house.

'Do you want to talk to me?' Again she hissed the question.

'Yes, in a word.'

'OK.' Then she turned. 'It's just Sandra. It's alright, Mummy.' She then turned to Yellich. 'Are you in a car?'

'Yes.'

'Which way you pointed?'

'Er . . . that way.' Yellich extended an arm to his left.

'OK. Drive away . . . take the first on the left . . . it's called Station Road, park just round the corner. If I'm not there in five minutes you can come back and arrest me.' She stepped back inside the house and closed the door. Yellich heard her shout, 'I'm going out for a bit, Mummy.'

Yellich walked down the drive and drove away. He turned into Station Road and waited, enjoying the summer foliage on the trees and the birdsong and the calm that is professional, middle-class, suburban York. A matter of moments later, Heather Lyall skipped round the corner and tapped on the passenger door of the car. Yellich opened the door and she slid into the passenger seat. He noticed that she had put on a lightweight summer cap and had changed her flip-flops for trainers but was otherwise dressed as she had been when she had opened the door to Yellich.

'Thanks,' she said. 'I reckon I owe you.'

'Oh, yes?'

'Yes . . . Dumb and Mad back there, all so very proper and what-will-the-neighbours-think? So I did something stupid once, brought the police to the door. Will they let me forget it? If Dumb knew you were a cop . . . well, stay and watch the fireworks, it would be like Vesuvius erupting.' She brushed her blond hair back with both hands and held it in a ponytail as she applied an elastic ribbon to hold it in place. 'So, what can I do for you?' She wound down the passenger-door window.

'Dunno really.' Yellich relaxed, he knew Heather Lyall was going to be co-operative. 'This is a bit like shooting fish in a barrel.'

'Shoot without proper aim in the hope that you might hit something?' She glanced at him with warmth in her eyes.

'Yep.'

She smiled. 'Rather like that image . . . shooting fish in a barrel. I think I'll use it, it's like that looking for men at a disco.'

'Well . . . Gary Sledge, Shane Sledge, Andy Styles, Chris Kingston and gang, Ray Pomfret, Ian Silcock, "Dutchy" Hollander, David Tebb, Jane Seymour, "Foxy" Stafford—'

'Don't . . .' Heather Lyall curled away from Yellich and put her hands up to her head.

'Sore point? I take it you recognize those names?'

'My father . . . that's the mad half . . .'

'I worked that out, thanks. Could be the mum half, though.'

'Well, Mad said I would never be able to free myself of my past . . . not fully . . . no matter how hard I try. No matter how hard you work to distance yourself from it, he said, your yesterdays are like body hair. You can shave, get rid of them for a day or two but they'll grow again and just as your body hair gets stronger as you grow older, so your yesterdays come to define your life as you get older. What you have done is as important as what you have become.'

'Quite a sage.'

'Well, it gets a bit tiresome at times, his homespun

philosophy but it's better than Sandra's dad with his Christmas-cracker humour. How she puts up with that, I don't know. You're Sandra, by the way.'

'I am?'

'So far as Dumb knows, I'm with Sandra.' She again glanced at him as she uncurled herself. 'Mind you, you don't much look like a Sandra.'

'I'm relieved to hear it, just as much as I am relieved that you didn't deny knowing the names I just mentioned.'

'Didn't know all of them.'

'Which did you know?'

'The Sledges.' She shook her head. 'It was them that got me into trouble . . . such a lovely leather jacket, all for me, wondered where he got the money. He being a "Tangy" . . . he didn't, did he? It was nicked, so I got nicked for receiving stolen goods.'

'And for shoplifting.'

'Read my file? Got lured into that. The Sledges, it was small fry for them, went into the shop . . . department store . . . the boys went off by themselves while me and this other girl, a hard nose from Tang Hall, only knew her as "Sylvia" . . . she was with Shane at the time, we went to the jewellery part of the shop and she slaps me, just like that, a real good slap across my face, called me a cow and started pulling my hair in the middle of the shop . . . no reason at all.'

'Decoy.'

'Yes, so I learned later. Anyway, we were rolling about, sending everything flying, a real catfight, people were looking, staff came from everywhere. Meanwhile, Shane and Gary were loading up carrier bags with goodies. They got stopped on the street, the store detectives were wise to the trick, and they had the four of us on CCTV the moment we stepped into the shop. Had footage of us talking as a group then separating into two pairs, kept one camera on the boys whilst me and this Tangy yclept "Sylvia" were turning the jewellery section upside down. So we was nicked, "Cor blimey, governor, bang to rights" as they say.'

'As they say.'

'So the relics were not best pleased: their very proper, convent-educated daughter, was done for receiving stolen goods and shoplifting. They confiscated my shoes for a month. House arrest, I dare say you could call it. Got fined by the York beaks. That's not the point though; it's a criminal record I have to declare on every job application. It's really working against me.'

'Shane Sledge gave the impression that you and Gary were an item.'

'Ha!' Heather Lyall flung her head back in derision. 'In his dreams. I would rather mate with a horned toad. I think the Sledges fancied Gary with me, add a touch of class to their clan down the Hall, but that is serious cloud cuckoo land . . . They're all bad news . . . I found out the hard way. I'm sorry about Gary. I heard it on the news and read the reports in the paper, but, as to involvement, not a chance.'

Yellich smiled. 'So you won't be averse to helping us then?'

'Nope. Well, I've got no loyalty to the Sledges, no matter what they might think. No loyalty to the police either. I'm impartial.'

'So you know the names I mentioned?'

'Not all of them.'

'Which did you recognize?'

'Well, the Sledges, of course . . . Andy Styles, met him a few times, he and Gary were good mates. They are the only ones I knew. Heard Hollander's name mentioned a time or two, they seemed frightened of him.'

'Do you know why?'

'He seemed to have a reputation as a dangerous person.'

'That all?'

'Yes . . . so I thought.'

'So, Hollander wasn't their enemy as such, he was more someone that they were wary of?'

'Well, yes, that seemed to be the case.'

'So why should they be wary of Hollander, unless they were either getting involved with him, or they were planning to go up against him?'

Heather Lyall shrugged.

'Any ideas?'

'Well . . . Gary felt he hadn't enough money to impress me. He thought it was all about money. He didn't seem to grasp that even if he won the lottery he wouldn't stand an earthly with me. I think he had a plan to extract money from Hollander. I think it involved photographs. The Sledges, Gary and Shane's father and his brothers, worked for Mr Hollander in some capacity . . . They had photographs of a girl and Hollander.'

Yellich's heart thumped.

'Do you recall the girl's name?'

'Namesake of one of Henry the Eighth's wives . . . All – Boys – Seek – Courteous – Honest – People.'

'What's that?'

'An aide-memoir. I was caught talking before grace when I was at school, in the first year, so Sister Mary told me to memorize the names of the wives of Henry the Eighth in the right order by the next morning, easy because Mad had taught me the usefulness of aide-memoires and how to devise them. So I worked that out and I can still remember it. Took me fifteen minutes. It's the first letter of the surname of his wives in their date order A. B. S. C. H. P., so . . . Catherine of Aragon, Anne Boleyn, Jane Seymour, Anne of Cleves, Kathryn Howard, Katherine Parr. Anyway, this girl and Hollander, she was one of those names.'

'Jane Seymour?'

'Sounds about right. Certainly wasn't Anne of Cleves.'

'Photographs exist showing Hollander and Jane Seymour together?'

'So I believe. I didn't see them, nor do I know where they are . . . or if, indeed, they exist at all.'

'Animal, vegetable or mineral . . .'

'What?'

'Nothing.' Yellich jotted details in his notepad. 'Just something me and my boss wondered. Now we know.'

'Vegetable, I'd say, if you are referring to the photographs.' Heather Lyall relaxed, seeming to Yellich to be enjoying the conversation as much as she enjoyed the sun upon her face. 'Poor Sister Mary, she thought she had had me stay up all night trying to remember something I worked out in fifteen minutes, silly old bat. Six Old Horses, Clumsy and Heavy, Trod on Albert.'

'What's that? Another aide-memoire, that's for sure, but what is it?'

'Sine over Opposite equals Hypotenuse, Cosine over Adjacent equals Hypotenuse, Tangent over Opposite equals Adjacent. Can't claim I thought that one up but it came in useful in the maths exam.'

'I can imagine.' Yellich thought how he had struggled to remember that rule. He could see the value of aide-memoires.

'Scout Masters Hate Eating Onions.'

'Oh, come on, I've a job to do.'

'The Great Lakes . . . Superior, Michigan, Huron, Erie, Ontario.' She smiled smugly. 'That's not original either, but it was useful in geography.'

Yellich committed it to memory. He thought Jeremy might just be capable of absorbing that, if not now, then at some point in the future. He was, after all, now tying his own shoelaces and was delighted to have mastered 'difficult' times, like twenty-two minutes past two. He could indeed be encouraged to remember the names of the Great Lakes of North America by that memory aid. It would, thought Yellich, be an achievement for his son and people, especially people like Jeremy, need achievements.

'My Very Easy Method Just Speeds Up Naming People.'

Yellich groaned. 'Go on.'

'The planets in the solar system, Mercury, Venus, Earth, Mars, Jupiter, Saturn, Uranus, Neptune, Pluto.'

Yellich pursed his lips. That too could be another one for Jeremy in a few years' time. 'Thanks,' he said. 'I know someone who might be able to use that.'

'Not original – I was taught that one as well, never used it, though, but it's in there in case I need to name the planets.'

'I am pleased for you. Now . . . come on . . . your help has been appreciated. Did you know Gary Sledge well enough to know where he'd hide the photographs of Jane Seymour and "Dutchy" Hollander? His flat was well turned over.'

'Oh, he wouldn't keep it there . . . he's too fly. That's a Tangy word, "fly". Out here in mummy-and-daddy-and-private-school-and-two-cars-in-the-drive land, we'd say "cunning" or "sly". You know, one of the sisters at the convent thought I was "sly". She actually wrote it on my end of term report. I took it as a compliment, though the relics were less than impressed.'

'So, where would Gary have hidden the photographs?'

'In plain sight.' She turned and smiled at Yellich.

'What?'

'I told you he was sly. He wouldn't hide them; he'd leave them in full view. Well, perhaps not quite full view, but they'd be more inclined to be in a photograph album rather than under the floorboards. They'd more likely be framed and hanging on the wall than be in a safety deposit box. That's the way Gary would have thought.'

'Hiding in plain sight,' Yellich repeated. 'Well, there was no photograph album in his drum nor were there photographs framed and hanging on the wall.'

'I didn't say there would be, but that was the way Gary thought.'

'When did you hear about the photographs?'

'At our trial. After I was arrested, Dumb and Mad forbade me to associate with the Sledges and I didn't, but we met at the trial and I walked over and said hello to them. It was then I heard about the plan Gary had to get some money. That's when I realized that he thought all he needed to win my favour was a lot of money. He was a real Tangy: "money answers everything".'

'So not at his flat. Where could they be?'

'Well, they'll be safe, that's for sure . . . and Gary would have had them duplicated, maybe even triplicated and he'll have kept the negatives especially safe.' She paused. 'Is there a reward?' She glanced at Yellich.

'No.'

'Poor little Gary was just not important enough. Is that it?'

'Possibly.'

'What about that girl . . . Jane what's her name? Any reward there?'

'I believe her parents did put up a reward . . . not much, about £5,000 . . . it may have been a grief response. I don't know if it's still offered.'

Heather Lyall smiled. 'Five big ones . . . travel, clothes. You know I could blow five big ones quite easily. It would be reward enough for me.'

'If you know something, you'd better tell me.'

'What? When I could sell it?' She winked at Yellich. 'Dog eat dog.'

'You could be prosecuted if you withhold information, especially involving an investigation of this magnitude.'

'Well, you know the nice thing about your fingerprints being taken is that they can only be taken once.' She reached for the door handle. 'I'll be in touch. Who do I ask for?'

'DS Yellich, Micklegate Bar Police Station.' She stepped out of the car. 'DS Yellich,' she said. 'D.S.Y. ... don't shout, yell, that'll do. D.S.Y., DS Yellich.' She turned and poked her head through the open window, somewhat over-confident, Yellich thought. 'It's just the way my little mind works.'

'So I have found out.'

'Richard Of York Gave Battle In Vain.'

Yellich sank backwards in the driving seat. 'What's that?'

'The colours of the spectrum: red, orange, yellow, green, blue, indigo, violet.'

'I know somebody who could make use of that as well.' He turned the ignition key.

'I'll be in touch. Who do I contact about the reward?'

'Don't shout, yell.'

'Your good self?'

'Yes. I'll find out for you.' He spoke dryly.

'When?'

'By this afternoon.'

'OK.' Heather Lyall tapped the open window frame of the door twice, as if to say goodbye, and was gone.

Hutton Cranswick Hennessey found to be a most pleasing village. He had alighted from the train and his first impression was passing favourable. The station itself was a small construction, just a platform on either side of the main line, each with a red bus-stop-style shelter. A main road with a level crossing abutted the station at ninety degrees to the tracks. Flat, open country lay to the east and although that particular day was still and warm, Hennessey could easily imagine the biting east wind slicing over those fields in January and February of the year. He stepped off the platform, crossed the tracks after the two-vehicle train had departed, unable to resist glancing to his left as the train moved further on its journey down a straight-as-an-arrow track which was lined with rich shrubbery on either side. The air smelled fresh, of the country, of the soil. He saw that, upon entering the village, he was on Main Street, on which lived the Seymour family. He glanced at the houses to his right and saw by their numbers that the Seymours lived towards the far end of Main Street. Hennessey encountered small shops, a line of them outside of which a group of mid-teenagers in jeans and trainers had gathered. He approached them, expecting to have to assert himself by walking through the group as they arrogantly stood their ground. He also expected comments to be thrown at him from good-humoured, to rude and obscene and anything in between, but as he approached, the group of teenagers melted deferentially to either side of the pavement and held an equally deferential silence as he passed. He realized he had worked in the city too long. Well-mannered children did still exist after all, not even as an endangered species as in the city, but were clearly thriving in the Yorkshire Wolds. To his left he saw a vast village green, quite the largest green he had ever seen, a walk across it would, he thought, occupy a full five minutes. There was a pond on the green with ducks, which were clearly used to humans, given the way they lazed contentedly while a man in a straw hat strolled close by them. The war memorial stood next to the duck pond, he saw, and then thought that the duck pond ought to be said to be next to the war memorial, so as to give the latter its place and due. Hennessey crossed the road, which was empty of traffic, and read the names on the memorial, as was his wont whenever he encountered a strange memorial.

He did it as an act of humility and also because of his interest in military history. He saw that the East Yorkshire Light Infantry, not surprisingly, was well represented among the named regiments, as were other Yorkshire regiments, the King's Own Yorkshire Light Infantry, the Duke of Wellington's Own particularly, but men of the village had evidently served, and fallen, with the Royal Engineers, the Royal Artillery and other units of the army. Yet others had given their lives in the service of the Royal Air Force and the Royal Navy. Interestingly, Hennessey noticed that one of the village's lost sons was a Home Guardsman. As a reader of war memorials, seeing a Home Guardsman's name carved with pride was unique in Hennessey's experience, and he wondered what had happened that a man too old or infirm for military service, or who was safe in a reserved occupation, should have given his life in the service of King and Country in the struggle against Nazism. He made a mental note of it; it would be a story to investigate during his looming retirement years. He was also pleased that the British Legion had been big-minded enough to allow the Home Guardsman's name to be included amongst the fallen heroes of Hutton Cranswick. A less generous-mindedness might have seen the man as 'not a proper soldier' and thus excluded his name. Such petty churlishness had clearly, and upliftingly, not applied in this case.

Hennessey recrossed the road and continued his walk up Main Street, past a small grocer's inside of which, by the sign outside, was the village post office, and came eventually to a house called 'Keeper's Lodge'. The house surprised him in that it was relatively recent, definitely late-twentieth century. He had, by its name and location on the main street of the village, expected a much older building. It was set back from the pavement by only a few feet behind a low brick wall, which was capped with narrow, concrete paving. The front door was wholly of opaque glass within the thin frame and held shut by a barrel lock. Clearly, the occupants of Hutton Cranswick were unfamiliar with burglary. As a police officer, with a police officer's eye, Hennessey looked at the door and despaired at the ease by which entry to the property could be forced: the lock would 'give' easily to a push, or alternatively a man-sized hole could equally easily be kicked in the glass. Polite teenagers and homes with this low level of security; he definitely had worked in the city too long. Were he not happy in Easingwold and were he possessed of the energy to cope with a house move, then relocation to Hutton Cranswick would, he thought, be more than inviting. It would be a real possibility. He opened the gate and within three steps he was at the door and pressed the bell.

As the 'ding dong' of the bell faded within the house, Hennessey took a step backwards and stood next to a green wheelie bin so as not to present too much of an intimidating presence on the threshold. Through the opaque glass he saw the figure of a woman approach the door and then, evidently seeing a tall, well-built male stranger on the other side of the glass, she stopped and turned, going into a room off the hallway. Moments later, a man in his middle years approached the door, said, 'Yes? Who is it?'

'Police,' Hennessey replied, pleased to see that some level of caution had been exercised.

'Police?'

'Yes.'

'What's it about?'

'Your late daughter, sir. Jane.'

'Jane? Our Jane?'

'Yes.' Hennessey reached into his jacket for his ID.

The man reached for the lock, turned it and opened the door cautiously. He blinked at Hennessey, who held up his identity card.

'You alone?' The man looked at Hennessey's ID.

'Yes.' He smiled what he hoped would be a reassuring smile. 'Just me.'

'Only the police have warned us about distraction burglaries, one guy keeps the householder chatting while the other burgles the house.'

'That has happened in this village?'

'Not yet, but it's been done in Driffield.'

'Well, as you see, I am a policeman.'

'And it's about Jane?'

'Yes.'

The man opened the door fully and stepped to one side. 'You'd better come in, Mr . . . ?'

'Hennessey.'

'From Beverley?' He was a short, silver-haired man.

'From York.' Hennessey stepped over the threshold of the house.

'Ah, bit like living in a museum, or so I hear.' Mr Seymour closed the door behind Hennessey. 'But we have lived in Hutton Cranswick all our lives, Betty and I. Born here, so I can't really say what living in York is like. If you'd care to go into the living room? That door there.'

Hennessey stepped into the living room. Mrs Seymour stood in the middle of the living room, hands clasped in front of her, smiling a welcome. She was a short woman with silver hair and warm, blue eyes. Hennessey saw an attractive young woman in her. The room was neat and, he thought, tastefully decorated, with a fitted carpet, solid-looking bookcase and sideboard in darkly stained wood, a modest television set, positioned discreetly in the corner, rather than commandingly away from the corner, a three-piece suite covered in green fabric. Prints of rural scenes hung on the wall. The window looked out on to a large and evidently well-tended rear garden, beyond and above which was the vast blue, and near cloudless sky.

'Please, Mr Hennessey, do take a seat. I'm Eric Seymour, this is my wife, Betty . . .'

'Pleased to meet you,' Hennessey smiled. The room smelled strongly of furniture polish. He sat on the settee.

'You say it's about our Jane?' Eric Seymour sat in one of the armchairs. Betty Seymour sat in the other.

'Yes.' Hennessey addressed Mr and Mrs Seymour, looking at each alternately, though, for some reason, he found himself more drawn to speaking to Mr Seymour and had to force himself to look at Mrs Seymour every few minutes. 'Really, there is little I can tell you. Nothing new has developed with regard to Jane's murder.'

'So you are still investigating?'

'It's a "sticker" . . . what we call a "sticker"; the investigation has run out of momentum but the case isn't closed, murder cases never are. What has happened is that another case seems to impinge on Jane's murder.'

'Really?'

'It's sometimes like that. It really seems to hinge on the extent of the involvement between Jane and "Dutchy" Hollander.'

'There was no involvement.' Eric Seymour spoke adamantly.

'None at all.' Betty Seymour sounded to Hennessey to be equally adamant.

'He was far too old for her and not a good man,' Eric explained, 'though we only learned about him after she reported him for what he did to her. The charge was indecent assault but that could mean anything . . . we'll never know what happened in that bedroom.' He glanced at the mantelpiece, at a framed photograph of a smiling girl wearing a riding hat and jodhpurs, sitting astride a black and white pony. 'She was thirteen when that was taken . . . her and Magpie. She was inconsolable when Magpie died. She never wanted another horse. Even as a young woman, she felt that Magpie was so special that no other horse could replace him. The thought of Jane having an involvement with that . . . that . . . person, no, no . . . no . . .' He shook his head. 'No, Jane would never countenance such a thing. Not our Jane.'

'She was at university in York, I understand?'

'Yes . . . she didn't wander too far from home. Her head teacher advised all the pupils who wanted to go to university to establish their independence by choosing a university that was far enough away to prohibit the temptation of coming home at weekends. So Jane's friends from school scattered to the four corners when they went to university . . . Swansea . . . London.'

'Canterbury,' added Betty Seymour. 'Remember that convent-educated girl whose family moved to the village and she joined Jane's year at the comprehensive school?'

'Oh yes, nice girl. Very well spoken.'

'She went to Canterbury, didn't stay the course . . . came back after the first couple of terms. Moved back in with her parents and then they moved into York. Can't remember her name . . .'

'Well, we didn't mind Jane staying close to home, suited us, she was our only child, she never actually left, but never actually moved back in either. During the long summer break that students get, she stayed in York. All those people from school came back to the village for the summers but Jane didn't, she had work in a pub . . . the Mail Coach.'

'The Mail Coach.' Hennessey reached into his jacket pocket for his notebook and ballpoint. As he did so, his mobile phone began to purr and vibrate. 'Excuse me.' He took the phone from his inside pocket. 'Don't like these things, but there is no denying their usefulness . . . ruin rail travel. Hello, Hennessey . . .' He fell silent as he listened, then he said, 'Well, I am actually with Mr and

Mrs Seymour now, I'll ask before I leave.' He switched off the machine. 'Don't want further interruptions. That was my sergeant, incidentally, working on the same case.'

'It's gratifying that the police haven't forgotten Jane. We'll never recover from her loss. We appreciate everything that you are doing.'

'As I said, murder cases are never closed. So Jane was living in a flat in York?'

'A shared house . . . down in Holgate. A lot of students rent houses in that part of the city. I remember the address, ninety Seagrave Walk, it's a cul-de-sac that backs on to allotments.'

'Did you visit her there?'

'No. We called to clear her room of her possessions.'

'Where are those possessions?'

'In her room. The police looked through them shortly after her body was found. They didn't take anything away, so I assume there was nothing of interest or relevance.'

'I'd like to take a look at them, anyway, if that's possible. A second look won't harm.'

'Of course.'

'Did you ever meet any of the people with whom she worked or lived at the time of her murder?'

'Only when we cleared out her room in York. That girl from the village was there . . .'

'Heather Lyall.' Betty Seymour beamed with pride. 'That was her name.'

Hennessey felt his jaw slacken. 'Heather Lyall,' he repeated. 'She was a friend of Jane's both here and in York in the summer she was murdered?'

'Yes. She had a room in the house in Seagrave Walk. Nice girl.' Eric Seymour stood. 'I'll show you Jane's room.'

Seymour led Hennessey up a narrow and, he found, a quite gently inclined set of stairs to a room at the rear of the house. The room boasted a skylight window as well as a main window, which had the same view as could be had from the living room, save from a slightly higher elevation.

'Jane loved this room.' Eric Seymour looked about him. 'It's as it was when she left our house for the last time. She used to lie in bed at night in the summer and look for shooting stars. She used to look up at the skylight window and shout out when she saw one. Anyway, things are as she left them and those cardboard boxes over there . . .' Seymour pointed to the corner of the room, 'those contain her possessions that we recovered from the house she lived in. I'll leave you . . .'

'Thanks.' Hennessey smiled. 'That would be appreciated.'

It was a disappointing trawl. Hennessey found nothing that pointed to Dutchy Hollander, or to any connection with Gary Sledge. The cardboard boxes contained her music collection of cassette tapes and CDs, her books – she had been, he noted, a student of history – as well as other personal items, a photograph album which showed her and her university friends, or her alone, snapshots and posed, but not one photograph showed either Hollander or the Sledge brothers. Her drawers contained clothing, in which Hennessey rummaged. He felt uncomfortable about probing the most private space of a deceased person but also knowing that items of great relevance are often hidden beneath or at the back of a drawer of clothing. Finding nothing, he ensured each drawer was reverentially pushed shut. He returned to the living room. 'I found nothing of interest,' he announced solemnly.

'Well, as I said, the original police team also searched her room and also found nothing,' Eric Seymour observed, 'but we won't be throwing anything away, just in case.'

'That would be helpful.' Hennessey paused. 'I'm sorry if this sounds a little . . . insensitive, but my sergeant who phoned just now . . . he has clearly been talking to someone who may have information—'

'Yes, it is,' Eric Seymour, said firmly.

'Sorry.'

'The reward, it is still extant. £5,000 if, in the view of the police, they receive information which leads directly to Jane's murderer's conviction, we will pay that person the sum of £5,000. It's all we have.'

'Just leaves us enough to bury ourselves,' Betty Seymour added. 'The house is rented, you see, it doesn't belong to us. We have no money in these bricks and this mortar.'

From Hutton Cranswick, Hennessey had returned to York, walked from the railway station up the gently inclined curve of Queen Street to Micklegate Bar Police Station. He signed in and walked to the CID corridor and sat at his desk and entered the recording of his visit to the Seymours in the file of the murder of Jane Seymour and cross-referenced it to the file on the murder of Gary Sledge. It was by then midday and he began to ponder where to take lunch, when the phone on his desk rang. He let it ring twice before picking it up and saying softly, yet authoritatively, 'DCI Hennessey.'

'Switchboard, sir, call from PC Boulton. He requests duty CID officer. There's really only yourself in the building, sir. DS Yellich is still out.'

'Very well.'

The line clicked and a youthful-sounding voice said, 'Hello, Boulton here.'

'Yes, Boulton, DCI Hennessey.'

'We have two suspicious deaths, sir.'

Hennessey groaned. 'Go on.'

'Two males, white European adults . . . member of the public contacted us, sir . . . we attended . . . two males appear to be deceased.'

'I see. What makes it suspicious?'

'Well . . . the fact that they are lying side by side and . . . nothing.'

'What do you mean, nothing?' Hennessey reached for his notepad and used his ballpoint to flip the page over.

'Well, just what I say, sir. Nothing . . . no sign of injury, no sign of violence . . . nothing about is disturbed. They are just lying there, side by side, as if asleep.'

'As if asleep,' Hennessey echoed and the initial report of Gary Sledge's body lying 'as if asleep' resonated in his memory. 'Where are you and have you requested the attendance of the police surgeon?'

'Yes, to the second question, sir, and we are near Sheriff Hutton . . . between Sheriff Hutton and West Willing.'

'Where's that? Nearest town?'

'There isn't one, really, sir.'

'How do I get there?'

'A64 towards Malton, sir. Look for the Flaxton turn-off to the left about six miles after leaving York . . . beyond Flaxton is West Willing.'

'Alright, I'll find it. What about SOCO? Have you alerted them?'

'Yes, sir.'

'Right. I'll be there a.s.a.p.' He replaced the receiver and walked to the enquiry desk and signed out and put 'Code 41? – Sheriff Hutton' beside his name. He saw the uniformed officer at the desk raise his eyebrows at the mention of 'Code 41' but said nothing. He left the building by the rear 'Staff Only' entrance/exit and strode across the car park to his car. Winding the window down to allow the interior of the car to 'breathe' in the heat, he drove out of the car park, joined the slow-moving traffic in the city centre and turned his car radio on to soothing Radio 4 and listened to a programme about giant crabs from Alaskan waters which had been introduced into the Barents

Sea as a food source and had clearly taken to their new home with relish. So much so that they are now being found in the waters off southern Norway, having destroyed the marine ecosystem along the route of their migration. The creatures were, concluded the programme, sounding like a weather front, 'expected in British waters soon'. Hennessey wondered if man would ever stop meddling with nature. He thought of the introduction of deer to New Zealand, rabbits to Australia, the French bees to England, all with disastrous consequences and now, by all accounts, holidaymakers in Scarborough and Bournemouth would soon be paddling amongst the crabs whose carapaces 'can be in excess of one metre wide'.

Then Hennessey concentrated on the drive and to the matter he was attending: two male corpses, suspicious circumstances, as if he and Yellich hadn't enough to cope with, with the Gary Sledge murder and the possible reawakening of the Jane Seymour case. It was, it seemed, as his lovely father often said, 'No rest for the wicked', and he knew he must, as his lovely father also often said, 'Carry on regardless'.

Seven

*in which a naïve youth gives much information to
his cost, a dangerous man is met and the gracious
reader learns of joy in Hennessey's life.*

MONDAY, 12.30 – 23.00 HOURS

Hennessey approached the village of Sheriff Hutton
driving slowly over the narrow, pasty grey road amid
flat fields, lush meadows and small stands of tall trees. He
saw the bustle of police activity in front of him, the white
patrol car with the blue light flashing, a little needlessly,
he thought, the black windowless mortuary van, a second,
unmarked car, the two white-shirted constables, the
turbaned Dr Mann, a shaken-looking member of the public
sitting on the verge with a small scarlet knapsack between
his knees, all under a vast blue and near cloudless sky.

He halted his car behind the mortuary van and, ensuring
the windows were fully wound down, he left it and walked
towards the constables, one of whom stepped forward as
he approached.

'Afternoon, sir.' The constable raised his right hand in
a token salute. He was youthful, fresh faced.

'Afternoon.' Hennessey nodded. 'You are . . . ?'

'PC Boulton, sir. This is PC Valleyfield.' Hennessey
and Valleyfield inclined their heads towards each other
as Hennessey brushed away an annoying fly.

'Plenty of those about, sir.' Boulton smiled. 'Freshly manured field close by, by the smell.'

'Yes . . .'

'And the bodies are beginning to thaw.'

'To thaw? You'd better show me what we've got.' He walked to where Dr Mann knelt beside a large sheet of black plastic. It clearly had been laid over the corpses. PC Boulton followed him.

Dr Mann stood as Hennessey approached. They greeted each other.

'Two males, white European adults, both deceased.' Dr Mann spoke solemnly. 'I pronounced death at 12.25 this day, just a few minutes ago. I suggest that the constable might like to request the forensic pathologist to attend.'

'I have done so, sir,' Boulton said in response to Hennessey's glance. 'She said she would attend directly.'

'Thank you.'

Dr Mann knelt and peeled back a corner of the sheet. Hennessey saw a particularly pale-looking face of a man in his early forties. He re-covered the face and peeled back the opposite corner of the sheet and revealed the face of the second man, similarly in his forties, similarly deathly pale. Dr Mann then re-covered the face of the second man. 'No apparent cause of death –' he stood – 'but noticeably cold. I suspect that they were frozen to death . . . it is an explanation . . . they are both clothed.'

'We haven't checked for any identification, sir,' Boulton offered. 'We didn't want to disturb the crime scene and there didn't seem to be any time pressure.'

'Quite right.' Hennessey's eye was caught by movement to his left, from the direction of Sheriff Hutton. He turned and allowed himself a smile as he saw two vehicles approaching. The leading vehicle he recognized.

'Scenes of Crime Officer, sir,' Boulton offered. 'I recognize the van . . . don't recognize the car, lovely old beast that is, Riley RME . . . early 1950s, I think.'

'R.M.A.,' Hennessey said, 'and it's 1947.'

'Really!' Boulton gasped. 'Lovely.'

'Yes, it's Dr D'Acre, the pathologist, you clearly haven't met her.'

'No, I haven't, sir. I've been where pathologists have attended but not met Dr D'Acre. I would have remembered the car.'

Hennessey watched the approach of the white Riley with red-painted mudguards. 'It's still in daily use.'

'Really, sir?' Boulton sighed. 'I bet that keeps it young.'

'Probably does, that and the regular servicing it receives.'

'You know the car, sir?'

'No, can't say I do. I've met Dr D'Acre a few times in situations like this. When we've been waiting for some reason, the conversation invariably turns to her Riley.'

'I see, sir.'

'I thought they were asleep, or resting in the sun.' The man scrambled to his feet as Hennessey approached. He seemed to Hennessey to be in his late fifties, short, silver hair, a neatly trimmed beard and moustache, both also silver.

'It happens.' Hennessey opened his notebook. 'A body lying as if at rest only becomes suspicious when the rest seems a little prolonged. Happened in York recently.'

'Really?'

'Yes, really. Every summer someone presumed sleeping on the beach or on a grassed area will in fact be deceased upon the beach or grass. You are Mr . . . ?'

'Crossford.' The man had a soft, seemingly learned voice to Hennessey's ears. He thought Crossford to be a retired professional man. 'I gave my details to the constables.'

'I see.'

Hennessey glanced around. He saw a cluster of rooftops on the southern skyline; they appeared to be the nearest buildings. He brushed another irksome fly from his face. 'Damn things.'

'Flies?' Crossford smiled. 'Lovely things, break down dung and provide food for birds and spiders. Frankly there wouldn't be many living things at all, including you and me, were it not for insects. They are at the bottom of the food chain, you see. Remove them and everything above them dies for want of sustenance . . . including you and me.'

'I dare say. So, you were walking?'

'Yes, bit too hot for it really, ought to have waited until the evening. I do eight miles near daily, keeps me in shape. So I do this walk three or four times a week. I like walking, it frees up the mind. Anyway, I saw those two, lying in the meadow side by side.'

'You approached them?'

'Yes. Just close enough to see that they didn't appear to be breathing and close enough to notice what appeared to be ice crystals in their hair and clothing.'

'Ice! In this weather?'

'Yes.' Crossford smiled. 'Suspicious or what? They could only have been dumped a few minutes before I came across them. And whoever dumped them wasn't afraid of them being found . . . look, ten feet from a public road. And no, I didn't see anything. Now, I was . . . I am walking from Sheriff Hutton towards West Willing. A fifteen-minute stroll will take you from one village to the other. No vehicle passed me in either direction between the time I put Sheriff Hutton behind me and the time I discovered the bodies. So the transport came from the direction of West Willing, dumped the bodies, or rather laid them neatly, and then drove away in the direction of West Willing. In other words, it turned round and drove back the way it had come. Whatever "it" was.'

Hennessey scanned the ground.

'No tracks,' Crossford said. 'Spent the time awaiting you looking for tracks or any other clues . . . nothing.'

'Useful, anyway. And you found the bodies at about . . . ?'

'At exactly 12.04 by my watch, which is kept accurate. Phoned three nines from my mobile. I saw only the remnants of ice on the bodies.'

'So the vehicle could have come via Sheriff Hutton?'

'No.' Crossford was adamant. 'I live in Sheriff Hutton, my house is on this road. Before I started the walk today, I spent an hour varnishing the fence at the front of my garden. I am convinced no vehicle passed in that time. I would have especially noticed a strange vehicle . . . a foreign vehicle.'

'Foreign?'

'I mean foreign to the area. Can't see a local person doing this, just wouldn't soil their own nest. Can't see it at all.'

'I can't either.'

'So the vehicle came from the direction of West Willing and went back in that selfsame direction, I would say.' Crossford leant forward and, showing what Hennessey thought to be great suppleness for a man of his years, swept up his knapsack and slid it over his right shoulder. 'I'll be on my way, if you have no further need of me. The constable has my details, as I said.'

'No further need at all. Thank you for alerting us. If you think of anything, anything relevant . . .'

'Of course. It's so true that relevance sometimes only becomes evident after a time delay. So, I'll bid you good day.' Crossford walked away, striding manfully, confidently, so Hennessey observed, towards West Willing.

Hennessey strolled over to where Dr D'Acre knelt beside one of the corpses.

'So far, I would concur with the police surgeon's assessment,' she said, aware of Hennessey's presence but not looking at him. 'They appear to have been frozen.' She pushed her right hand under the body. 'Yes, very chilled on the underside. Haven't been here very long. They have been frozen but whether that caused death, whether freezing was post or ante mortem, I can't say. There was nothing to suggest it was post mortem. No evidence of injury at all. Well, I can do the PM this afternoon, if they can be removed?'

'SOCO hasn't taken photographs yet, sir,' PC Boulton advised, keenly.

'Very well.' Hennessey smiled his thanks. 'As soon as the photographs have been taken, the bodies can be taken to York District, Department of Pathology.'

'Very good, sir.'

Dr D'Acre stood and stepped away from the corpses, allowing the SOCO officers to advance with their cameras. 'Haven't taken a rectal or soil temperature yet.' She turned to Hennessey. 'I'll have to do that before they are taken away . . . have to remove the clothing to facilitate that.'

'Of course.'

'So, photographs first.'

'Indeed. Then identification. I have a sudden feeling that I know who they are.'

'Will you be observing the post-mortem for the police, Chief Inspector, after they have been identified? If you are correct.'

'Yes, I think so. Sergeant Yellich is engaged today.'

'Intriguing,' Dr D'Acre commented as the bulb in the Scenes of Crime Officer's camera flashed. She glanced at the bodies.

'What is?'

'This murder, for murder it is. It has a certain style. We have very classy murders in the Vale of York. I have commented thus before, and I comment again, not for us the grubby set-tos that go too far, that they have in South

Yorkshire. There is style in our murders . . . and such pleasant surroundings too. I was a locum pathologist in Sheffield once, never again. Cleaner than it once was, as a city I mean, but never worked in a setting as pleasant as this and a case as intriguing as this. Two bodies laid side by side probably, highly probably, murdered by being frozen. Intriguing.'

'Just left them there, boss. Out in the sticks.'

'Nothing to tie you to them?' Hollander pulled on the cigar.

'No, boss.' The taller man spoke. 'Just left them by the side of a road . . . middle of nowhere. We did a three-point turn and came back to York. Didn't see any other vehicles until we were on the main road again. And nobody saw us.'

'Sure?'

'Positive.'

George Hennessey and Emily Pomfret sat in a heavy silence. A highly polished bench ran round three sides of the room, broken only by the door through which he and Mrs Pomfret had entered. The fourth wall was occupied by a thick, velvet curtain in sombre maroon, beside which was a second door. Having advised Mrs Pomfret that it wouldn't be like what she may have seen in films, that the body wouldn't be pulled out of a bank of drawers and a sheet peeled back to reveal his face – it would be like looking at him sleeping, he had said – and then with nothing left to offer, he and Mrs Pomfret sat adjacent to each other, and waited. Then eventually, there came from behind the curtain a soft, mechanical clicking sound, then a further period of silence, as if in apology for the clicking sound having been made. The second door beside the curtain opened and a solemn-faced nurse entered. She looked at Hennessey, who nodded. The nurse then pulled a cord

beside the curtain downwards with a hand-to-hand movement, which caused the curtains to part silently. Hennessey
approached the large pane of glass, which was revealed
by the parting of the curtains. He quietly beckoned Mrs
Pomfret to stand beside him. She did so slowly with, he
thought, clear and understandable reluctance.

The pane of glass revealed Raymond Pomfret lying on
a hospital trolley. He was neatly and tightly wrapped in
starched white sheets and his head was similarly band-
aged in white, with only the face showing. By some deft
use of light and shade nothing else was visible, giving the
impression that the deceased was floating, peacefully
asleep, in an unfathomable blackness. It was, Hennessey
had often believed, as sensitive a display of a loved one
that could be had.

'Yes,' Mrs Pomfret nodded, speaking slowly as if,
Hennessey wondered, she was more sedated than was usual.
'That's Raymond. My husband.' She turned to the door.

'I'll have someone drive you home,' Hennessey offered.

'I'd rather walk. Thanks.'

Hennessey nodded his thanks to the nurse, who closed
the curtains and swiftly exited the room via the second
door. In the anteroom Emily Pomfret hurried past a
worried-looking woman who sat in an armchair. Neither
woman glanced at each other. Hennessey shut the door of
the viewing suite behind him and waited until Mrs Pomfret
was out of earshot and then looked at the seated woman
and said, 'Mrs Silcock, if you'd care to step into this room,
please.'

'Sorry about the delay.' Louise D'Acre sat in the chair in
front of her small desk in her small, cramped office adjacent to the pathology laboratory in the York District
Hospital. 'Dr Leach should be finished soon.'

'No matter.' George Hennessey sat in an upright chair

which stood beside Dr D'Acre's desk. 'It's nice to be in the cool for a change. Pleasant weather can be a little unpleasant on occasions. I prefer to keep warm in cold weather than to have to keep cool in hot weather.'

'Yes, my daughter Dianne ... the eldest ... she announced yesterday that she'd prefer the same. She said she'd prefer two weeks in Scotland in January to two weeks in the Mediterranean in July, quite mature thinking for a fifteen-year-old. All her friends can't wait to go on holiday as a gang without their parents and are poring over package holiday brochures. Mind you, it may have been a reaction to having spent the afternoon mucking out Samson ... very hot, sweaty, tiring work. I can see how a couple of weeks on a glacier might seem appealing after that.'

Hennessey smiled. 'How are your other children?'

'Daniel's climbing trees, I expect. He's with his father for a couple of weeks. Fiona's away with the French Club.'

'The French Club?'

'Well, as the name suggests, it's a club run by her enthusiastic French teacher. They meet once a week at lunchtime and converse in French in small groups, open to any pupil who wants to master the language ... wants to give it more than lessons and homework ... and each summer the French Club goes on a three-week inexpensive camping holiday near Calais, just across the Channel, but that's all you need. The purpose is not to visit France per se but to immerse themselves in the language, to make it come alive.'

'Good idea.'

'Yes, it is. The final-year pupils have their own short and small camp during the Easter break, just a few weeks before their final, qualifying exams.'

'So it's just you and Dianne at home?'

'Not even her now. I kissed her goodbye this morning.

She's gone to join her brother with their father. She delayed going as much as she could. She had the usual difficulty, dragging herself away from the stables . . . that I expected, but this year there seemed to be an additional reluctance.' Louise D'Acre was a trim, slender woman, short hair, with just a trace of pale lipstick. Her lithe body movements would have told an astute observer of a strong body of well-toned muscle.

'Oh?'

'Yes, I suspect that things between her and her father are . . . strained. Alexander and Dianne never really saw eye to eye from day one. She was a headstrong girl before she could walk and he can be equally stubborn. They'll both have dug their respective heels in about an issue to which I am not privy, waiting for the other to relent. Anyway the old house is big and quiet at the moment.'

Hennessey attempted eye contact but Louise D'Acre very purposefully avoided it.

'He'll be finished in a minute. Dr Leach, I mean.'

'Another murder?' Hennessey asked, sensitive to the change of subject.

'Yes, a relatively elderly man, in Harrogate, of all places, genteel Harrogate. The couple retired to Harrogate after nearly forty years of a successful marriage. She couldn't cope with him being in the house all the time, nothing but arguments, so Dr Leach told me. Then this forenoon she grabbed and lunged and plunged. He is upon ye slab, she is in ye lockup and in floods of tears, by all accounts.' She looked up at the open doorway of her office. 'Yes, Eric?'

Hennessey turned, he saw the smiling Eric Filey standing there.

'Dr Leach sends his apologies, ma'am,' Filay announced deferentially. 'The pathology laboratory is free now.'

'Thank you.' Dr D'Acre returned the smile. 'Myself and

Mr Hennessey will be along directly.' She glanced at Hennessey. 'Shall we go?'

Two hours later Hennessey walked leisurely away from York District Hospital, grateful for the shade offered by the brim of his Panama, and carrying his jacket over his arm. The city baked, the narrow streets seemed to him to trap the heat and he found brief respite by taking a short cut through one or two snickelways, the small, narrow passages that interlace the medieval part of the city, like a street system within a street system. In the pedestrian precincts, people thronged, day-trippers in the main, he thought, who looked about themselves as they walked, but also many locals who went knowingly about their business, looking straight ahead. Two young women in long cheesecloth skirts played expertly upon the violin, filling their part of Castlegate with sweet music. Further along the pavement, a young man shouted, rather than sang, in accompaniment to a guitar, and yet further along, a young man sat with his knees under his chin beside a sign written on cardboard which read 'HUNGRY HOMELESS, PLEASE HELP'. Each person or persons had a collection hat in front of them and were, in Hennessey's view, 'deserving, less deserving and undeserving', in that order, but at least he felt himself thankful that the beggar didn't have a puppy tethered on the end of a length of string to evoke sympathy. He dropped a coin in the hat of the girls who filled the air with a sweet violin duo; the guitar player and the beggar he studied with a policeman's eye. They both, he thought, had the look about them of someone who had known the inside of a police station. He didn't recognize either and so walked on.

So . . . frozen to death. It had been a speedily conducted post-mortem on both bodies. Mr Silcock and Mr Pomfret had no injuries or marks upon their bodies that could

138

explain the cause of death. Blood samples had been sent to the Forensic Science Laboratory at Wetherby for toxicology tests, but Dr D'Acre's opinion was that should the toxicology tests prove negative, as she believed they would so prove, then death was caused by freezing. Hypothermia. 'Not a bad way to go really, once the initial pain wears off as the nerve endings become numb,' she'd said. 'The body pulls all the blood into the chest cavity to insulate the heart and the lungs and liver and kidneys, tries to keep the vital organs functioning, but it doesn't recognize the brain as a vital organ and so one's last moments of consciousness are moments of a profound sense of calm and well being.' Anticipating Hennessey's question as he peeled off the surgical gloves, she'd added, 'People who have been rescued at the last minute, they all report the same sense of well being after feeling cold and frightened. I dare say it would have been the same for the two gentlemen before they finally succumbed, frozen from the outside in and thawed from the outside in. The internal organs were still fairly solid.'

Hennessey had asked what could have caused such freezing.

'Locked in the centre of an iceberg.' Dr D'Acre had smiled. 'That would have done the job, but in York and its environs, midsummer . . . a deep freeze with the thermostat turned down as low as low could be, and they would probably have been kept therein for a minimum of twelve hours.'

After receiving Dr D'Acre's assurance that her report would be faxed to him tomorrow, Hennessey strolled back to Micklegate Bar Police Station through the crowded streets of central York, past street performers and beggars, deserving, less deserving and undeserving.

He signed in at the enquiry desk and checked his pigeon-hole. There was nothing of import. He saw only the routinely sent circular asking all officers to use second-class stamps, write on both sides of a piece of paper and make all phone calls after 2 p.m. whenever possible. There was notification of the retirement party for one Inspector North. Hennessey hardly knew the man and while he would contribute to his retirement gift, he doubted that he would attend the party; a third circular, that the divisional underwater search team was relocating to new premises. He took the circulars away with him and, in his office, consigned them to the wastepaper basket. He sat at his desk and reached for the missing persons' files on Raymond Pomfret and Ian Silcock. Before he could write up the initial findings of the post-mortem, Yellich tapped on his doorframe.

'Thought I heard you come in, boss.'

'Yes . . . sorry I didn't get back to you sooner about that reward, it's still extant. Delightful couple . . . the money's all they have, I really wouldn't like to see them part with it but, if it leads to a conviction . . .'

'Yes, I wouldn't really like little Miss Lyall to receive it. I can think of more deserving cases.'

'Really? What information did she give?'

'Good information.' Uninvited, Yellich sat in the chair in front of Hennessey's desk. 'She told me what was likely to be the reason for the search of Gary Sledge's flat . . . photographs.'

'Of?'

'Jane Seymour and Dutchy Hollander . . . probably. She emphasized "probably" but she was certain enough to ask about the reward, hence my phone call.'

'So, Gary Sledge had photographs of Jane Seymour and Hollander?'

'Is the implication.'

'And who would want to assume possession of said photographs?'

'Dutchy Hollander. It blows his alibi for the murder of Jane Seymour. He has signed a statement that he didn't know her at all.'

'That could backfire on him.' Hennessey put his pen on the file. 'I thought that earlier.'

'Could very easily.'

'Did she . . . what was her name . . . Lyall?'

'Heather Lyall, yes, sir.'

'Did she indicate where the photographs might be?'

'She said that Gary was a cunning, sly young man, that he would hide things in plain sight.'

'So they wouldn't be buried somewhere, they'd be in a photograph album, that sort of plain sight?'

'So we ask the Burton and Stafford crew if they were looking for photographs. They'll co-operate, they're scared of the Sledge family.'

'Where are they?'

'Full Sutton.'

'OK. You could perhaps do that this afternoon?'

'Yes, boss. The reason I came to see you is that there has been a development in the Pomfret case.'

'Already! I've just come from the post-mortem.'

'Yes, sir. Uniforms picked up a youth, tried to obtain money using a credit card, couldn't give the bank staff the correct name. They wanted the cardholder's mother's maiden name. He couldn't give it, so the bank staff held on to the card and he made a speedy exit. They called us, handed the attending officer the card and gave a good and detailed description. The officers found him, rapidly so.'

'You're going to tell me the card belonged to Raymond Pomfret.'

'Yes.' Yellich nodded. 'The youth was also in possession of a wallet belonging to one Ian Silcock. The collator fed the name into the computer. Both came back known with your good self as the interested police officer.'

'Interested is the word.'

'Where is he? In the cells?'

'Yes, sir.' Yellich stood. 'Harvey Longfellow by name.'

'Longfellow.' Hennessey also stood. 'Could never see the appeal in him. Henry Wadsworth that is . . . not Harvey. Anyway, lead on and introduce us.'

Harvey Longfellow struck Hennessey as being a timid youth. He had given his age as eighteen years, which seemed to Hennessey to be accurate. He was slight and slender and had a look of worry in his eyes. Hennessey liked that. It spoke, he thought, of honesty. Here, he thought, here was a youth, most probably not of criminal intent, who had strayed on to the wrong side of the law, who would be frightened by the experience and who would not stray again. Hopefully, here, he further thought, was a youth who would co-operate. Hopefully. He stood reverentially as Hennessey and Yellich entered the cell.

'Obtaining money by deception –' Hennessey spoke softly – 'and theft. First time in trouble with the law?'

'Yes, sir.' Longfellow nodded. His voice quaked.

'We'll check anyway, but the rule is, if you scratch our back, we'll scratch yours. You help us, we'll help you.'

'You can get me off?'

'No. All we can do is put a word in for you. Let the magistrates know you helped us, let the parole board know you helped us.'

'Parole . . .' Longfellow's voice shook. 'I'm going to prison?'

'It's a possibility.'

'What do I say?'

'The truth.' Hennessey thought with some force that his was ironically and hypocritically not a truthful answer. The truthful answer would be 'nothing'. 'Cough to nowt' is the rule; answer 'no comment' to every question. But Hennessey needed information and he was prepared to give bad advice in order to get it. If Harvey Longfellow was a little more streetwise, he would claim to having found the credit card and the wallet in the street and had picked them up. That might indeed have been the case; Hennessey hoped it wasn't. 'Myself and Mr Yellich here, we are not interested in your attempting to obtain money with the credit card, or being in possession of the wallet.'

'You are not?' Longfellow was dressed all in yellow. A yellow T-shirt, a yellow jacket, yellow trousers . . . it was easy to see why the bank staff had been able to describe him so accurately and the police pick him up so rapidly. If Longfellow was embarking on a criminal career, which Hennessey hoped for Longfellow's sake that he was not, then the boy clearly had much to learn, and avoiding conspicuous appearance is the first lesson.

'No, we are not. If we were, we'd be in an interview room talking on the record, not here, talking off the record.'

'That's in my interest, to talk off the record?'

'Yes.' Hennessey nodded, and that, he thought, was at least true. Keep as much as you can off the record, that's another of the unwritten rules of survival among those of criminal bent. 'What we want to know is how you came across the wallet and credit card. So tell us.'

'It'll help me?'

'Yes. If you don't dig yourself into a hole by telling lies.'

'I took them from the dead bodies.'

Hennessey sighed with relief; beside him he sensed Yellich felt similar relief. The beggar he had passed whilst walking back from the hospital would, he felt, doubtless have found them while 'searching the waste bins for my supper' but Longfellow was clearly still possessed of some trace elements of childish sense of fairness.

'OK. So you saw the bodies being dumped out by Sheriff Hutton?'

'Yes.'

'What were you doing out there?'

'I live out that way.'

'Farm worker?'

'No . . . can't get work, live with Mum . . . not a lot of money. I was in the woods setting snares for pheasants and rabbits.'

'Poaching?'

'Yes.'

'You can go to gaol for that.'

'I know, but it's the only fresh meat we get. Out there, tins are expensive, twice as expensive as in the town. So I take a pheasant or a rabbit, sometimes a hare.'

'You went poaching in those clothes?'

Longfellow smiled. 'Think I'm soft in the head? No, I was dressed in a green vest and camouflage trousers and boots. I came home and changed into my city clothes . . . the Yellow Peril, that's what the man said I'd be, "the Yellow Peril".'

'Who said that?'

'The man in the open market near the Shambles, he sold me the clothes, said I'd attract all the girls, that I'd get known as "the Yellow Peril". Doesn't seem to be working. Not yet anyway.'

'OK. So what did you see?'

'Saw a yellow pickup, Leyland Sherpa front.'

'Yellow?'

'Yes, like my clothes . . . yellow cab, yellow body . . .'

'OK.'

'Ducked down. Thought at first it was estate workers, or the gamekeepers. The man who owns that land, he doesn't like his game being taken, even if it's just the rabbits who do a lot of damage. I was frightened but I kept watching. Two guys stopped the pickup by the side of the meadow, took a cover off the back and carried two bodies from the pickup into the meadow and left them, went back to the pickup, turned it round and went back the way they'd come . . . went back to West Willing, well, went back *towards* West Willing.'

'Then?'

'Then I broke cover, went to the bodies . . . They were frozen . . . all ice . . . There was nobody about, so I went through their pockets, found a wallet in one and just a credit-card holder in the other man's pocket.'

'And watches and other valuables?'

Longfellow shrugged. 'They're at home. Gave some money to my mum, she went into the village to buy food. We'd be eating properly for the first time for a long time. My snares haven't been too good, not for a while. Tinned Irish stew doesn't really fill you up.'

'And the rest of the money?'

'Only kept a few quid, I needed the bus fare into York. I wanted to use the plastic card to get money from the bank. I'd heard you could do that. Then they started asking what my mum's maiden name was, so I told them. Then they said they'd hold on to the card. Then I ran because I sensed something was up, but I told them "Pool". My mum was Miss Pool before she married my dad, so I gave them the right answer but they still suspected something, so I ran. Got stopped by the cops ten minutes later.'

Hennessey thought: Much to learn indeed.

'This is helping me?'

'Yes. Just tell the interested officer what you've told us. You should emphasize that you stole so you and your mum could eat.'

'OK.'

'You'll have a solicitor present when you are inter- viewed. He or she will keep you right.'

'OK.' Longfellow smiled.

'Would you recognize the men in the pickup?'

'Probably, I got a real good look. One was really well built, frizzy hair, beard, beer belly but strong – he did all the lifting. The other was smaller, younger, clean-shaven, short hair. He looked very serious, like he never laughed, never laughed at nothing.'

'This is good, Harvey. Any markings on the van?'

'Yes . . . Dillet Builders.'

'Dillet?' Yellich wrote in his notebook.

'Yes, in black on yellow on the side door, Dillet Builders, York.'

'Thanks, Harvey, this has really helped us. We'll have to take a formal statement from you later, but this is good.' Hennessey smiled. 'Very good.' He tapped on the cell door. 'Have to leave you now, but this is good, Harvey. Thanks.'

Walking down the corridor to the stairs which would take them up to the ground floor of the police station, Yellich said, 'He's going down.'

'Yes.' Hennessey nodded. 'Looting, worst of all types of theft, he'll be lucky to escape a prison sentence. You know part of me wanted to tell him to say he found the wallet and credit card. He's not evil, he's stupid . . . he won't survive in prison.'

'I know what you mean, skipper.'

'But we have to take a statement from him about what he saw, and what he did, so that's it. He might be able to negotiate an early parole but he is going to be a guest of Her Majesty, that's all but certain. So, for action?'

'Well, I'm going to Full Sutton to interview the Burton and Stafford crew. That'll take the rest of the day.'

'Ah, yes.'

'I'll look up Dillet Builders. We'll rendezvous in my office tomorrow at 08.30.'

'Very good, sir.'

'I'm going to pay a call on Mr Hollander.'

'Is that wise, sir?' Yellich paused to allow Hennessey to ascend the narrow staircase.

'Yes . . . I'll be safe. I'll ensure that he knows that my colleagues know where I am.'

'Good.' Yellich followed Hennessey up the stairs.

'I want to meet him, heard so much about him, I want to make his acquaintance. I want to rattle his cage.'

'Rattle his cage?' Yellich chuckled as he echoed the phrase.

'It is, I believe, a Scottish expression. At least I first heard it from a Scot, a Glaswegian shipmate from my days in the Navy, Tam Galloway by name. Insisted on addressing everyone as "Jimmy". Anyway we were in "The Gut" in Valletta, Malta, a bar owner was throwing a tantrum in the street and Tam said, "Someone's rattled his cage." It was the first time I had heard that expression. I still think it's as amusing now as I did then. Glaswegians have a particularly punchy way of talking. I have observed so over the years, and that is but one example. So I will go and introduce myself to Dutchy Hollander . . . rattle his cage. See you tomorrow.'

Dutchy Hollander's yellow house, Hennessey found, stood in expansive grounds to the west of York. It was, he thought, Edwardian, perhaps about a hundred years old, in grey brick . . . a style which had cleaner lines than the cluttered lines beloved of Victorian architects, yet seemed to Hennessey to be unsure of itself in some way. It was a style of house which clearly anticipated early and mid-twentieth-century design but lacked a certain confidence of appearance, so Hennessey thought as he surveyed it from the road. The grounds were bounded by freshly painted yellow railings; the gateway had an intercom to facilitate access. Hennessey got out of his car and pressed the intercom bell. He waited for some moments, during which he further surveyed the house. Two cars were parked in front of the house, both black, both highly polished and glinting in the sun. Outbuildings stood at each side of the house. The line of railings could be seen fully encompassing the house at varying distances but never closer, thought Hennessey, than the length of a football pitch. Hollander was clearly a man who liked his own territory. He pressed the button again. He waited again. Then a crackly voice said, 'Yes?'

'Mr Hollander, please.'

'Who wants to see him?'

'Police.' Hennessey could not tell if the voice was male or female.

'Wait a minute.'

Female, he thought. Harsh, made harsher by the intercom system. He would doubtless soon find out. He looked again at the house. At the gateway he was thus some distance from the house, but nevertheless couldn't discern any security system, no telltale white box high on the wall, for example. He thought it curious. He wondered what form of security Hollander had opted for because there was nothing in evidence save for the railings, and they wouldn't keep out a determined felon. They certainly didn't prevent Jane Seymour from scaling them when she escaped from Hollander's party.

'Hello?' the female voice crackled again.

'Yes . . . still here.' Hennessey pressed the button, which was clearly labelled 'press to speak'.

'What's it about?'

Hennessey paused and thought: Mild curiosity and multiple murder and everything else in between, but said, 'Let's just say it's important enough for me to come back with a warrant and an army of constables if need be, or Mr Hollander can let me, and me alone in, to talk in a civilized manner.'

'Wait . . .'

Hennessey waited.

And waited.

He watched a heron fly low over the grounds of Hollander's house.

He glanced up at the vapour trail of a jet airliner as it flew from east to west, from continental Europe to North America. He fancied the window-seated passengers looking down upon the green and pleasant.

'Hello . . .' the voice crackled.

Hennessey pressed the button. 'Yes, still here. Not going anywhere . . . unless I have to and then it will be only in order to come back.'

'Mr Hollander says to come in but watch the dogs. Stay in your car until the dogs have been taken away.'

Dogs . . . Hennessey knew there had to be something.

'What . . . ? Didn't hear . . .'

Nothing. He released the button and walked back to his car as the gates swung silently open.

Hennessey drove down the long, straight drive towards Hollander's house. Here, he thought, here the Victorians would have made the drive slightly curved, tree lined, with a small lake off to one side. In his rear-view mirror he saw the gates close behind him and although he disliked them, he was suddenly and unexpectedly reassured by the presence of his mobile phone in his jacket pocket. As he drove up to the house, a Dobermann ran round the corner of the house, then a second, and a third . . . then more . . . six in all, all running towards his car, snarling, barking. He slowed and drove the remainder of the way to the front of the house with his car surrounded by a growling pack of black and tan beasts. He halted his car in front of the front door and waited until some person or persons appeared to take control of the animals. He pondered that with security like that, and the dogs, it was little wonder that Hollander had no need of a burglar alarm, but then further pondered that no security system is foolproof. Indeed, had he not more than once in his career come across guard dogs subdued by nothing more complicated than a fish and chip supper, or similar?

A man appeared, walking from the side to the front of the house, walking at his own pace, on his own terms. He was, thought Hennessey, a man in his fifties, hard eyes, the look of 'inside' about him. He viewed Hennessey with clear and evident distaste and then put a whistle to his lips and blew. Hennessey didn't hear anything, though the dogs clearly did for they instantly stopped barking and slunk behind the man. Hennessey remained in his car.

The front door of the house opened. A tall, gaunt-looking woman, and nervous too, thought Hennessey, stood on the threshold. She glanced at the man who had controlled the dogs and then walked towards Hennessey, who wound down his window as she neared him. 'Police?' she asked.

Hennessey nodded and showed her his ID.

'Follow me, please. The dogs won't attack you.'

Hennessey stepped out of the car, keenly aware of six pairs of hungry Dobermann eyes watching his every move, as if waiting for the slightest signal or excuse to attack. He tried to evince no fear but was pleased when he stepped into the cool of the foyer and the main door was shut behind him with a heavy 'clunk'.

'If you'd like to follow me, please?' The woman's voice was husky. Hennessey assumed that it had been she who had responded to his pressing the button of the intercom on the gate. She was slender, was probably a beauty in her youth but now, silver-haired, furrowed brow, she was most probably retained as an efficient manager of the household, rather than any other reason, so was Hennessey's first impression. She walked on, clicking heels across the tiled hallway of the house to a door which stood off to the left. She opened the door with a flourish, stepped into the room and said, 'The police, Mr Hollander.' She stepped aside and allowed Hennessey to enter the room.

Hennessey walked into the room and he and Hollander looked at each other, sizing each other up as adversaries do upon initial encounter and Hollander smiled, grinned even, as if to say, 'I win.' He then glanced at the gaunt, silver-haired woman and said, 'Thank you, Emily.' Emily dutifully withdrew.

Hennessey could see why Hollander allowed himself to smile: he seemed to win on all points. The two men were about the same age and he was clearly more successful than Hennessey in terms of monetary wealth, if nothing else. The house, the contents of the room alone, the designer clothes, the rings on his fingers, the gold pendant round his neck, the gold-plated cigarette holder, the Balkan Sobranie 'Black Russian' cigarette, held in said holder. The shiny shoes, compared to Hennessey's dulled shoes after a day's work and a walk in the dusty streets of York; the neatly pressed cavalry twill trousers, compared to Hennessey's tweedy 'bags'; the silk shirt, compared to Hennessey's cotton shirt, and polyester jacket; the coiffure compared to Hennessey's straggly hair, in need of another trim from the barber's in the village – when he had an hour to spare.

'Mr . . . ?'

'Hennessey. Detective Chief Inspector, Micklegate Bar Police Station, York.'

'Ah . . .' The glint of gold in Hollander's mouth just had, thought Hennessey, just had to be there, so much so that if it wasn't, the man's image would be incomplete.

'Chief Inspector, I'm sorry, to what do I owe the pleasure?' He indicated a deep and comfortable-looking armchair. 'Please, won't you have a seat?'

Hennessey accepted the invitation, if only because he

had learned from experience that it is much easier to read a room from a sitting position. Being seated, he had found, allows one to move one's head from side to side a little more discreetly. When standing, he found he seemed to be obliged to keep his eyes fixed upon the person to whom he was talking. Hollander also sat. Beside his chair was a small table upon which stood an ashtray. Hollander placed his cigarette in the ashtray and allowed it to smoulder, taking no further interest in it.

'We're investigating a murder,' Hennessey said.

'We, or you?'

'I am sorry?'

'I always thought police officers, detectives at least, visited in pairs. I see you are alone.'

'This is a one-handed visit. It's not quite the same as being alone – my colleagues know where I am.'

Hollander nodded almost imperceptibly.

'And how may I help you?'

'Me . . . minimally, but the police, you can help the police greatly.'

Hollander smiled. Hennessey felt that Hollander was beginning to get wary of him. Hollander clearly felt he had won on turn-out, on appearance, but Hennessey further sensed that Hollander felt he had lost on points when it came to brain on brain, mind on mind.

'The murder of Gary Sledge.'

'Who?'

'Wednesday last, found near the walls.'

'Oh, yes . . . I read it; saw it on the local news as well. That did seem unfortunate.'

'You knew him?'

'I did?' Hollander's eyebrows rose.

'You know his family. His father and his father's brothers do some work for you . . . or did . . . probably still do.'

'They do?'

'So we are to believe . . . strong men . . . muscle men . . . minders . . . hit men, perhaps?'

Hollander held up his right hand. 'I am a legitimate business man, Mr . . . Detective Chief Inspector. I'm in property. I know the property business inside out.'

'But the link with the family is there.'

'I employ many people.'

'Not always wisely, it seems.'

'Meaning?'

'Well, if you hired someone to torture and then murder young Mr Sledge, you didn't hire wisely. You see, the two men you hired, Pomfret and Silcock . . .' Hennessey enjoyed watching colour drain from Hollander's face. 'Oh yes, we traced them, they were given up by the boys they subcontracted to help them, those lads are more frightened of the Sledge family than they are of . . . well, anyone else. They coughed, gave up Pomfret and Silcock. They are now in police custody, protective custody at their own request. They don't know who hired Pomfret and Silcock, though.'

Hollander smiled, seemingly relieved.

'Then lo and behold . . . Pomfret and Silcock are reported missing.'

'Shame.'

'Oh, but they turned up, deceased, but they turned up. Doubtless you'll read that in the papers or see the item on the TV local news . . . frozen to death, lying in the middle of a field by the side of a road out in the Vale. Still cold on a day like this.'

'Imagine.'

'Well, we have a witness.'

Hollander paled again. 'Well . . . good for you.'

'It is very useful.'

'Who is this witness?'

Hennessey smiled. 'Now, that would be telling but he
. . . or she . . . or they, are in protective custody at the
moment. It's interesting that you ask, though.'

'Just interested.'

'Why?'

Hollander shrugged.

'Well, it gives us something to go on.' Hennessey moved
the conversation on. 'I understand Mr Silcock worked for
you?'

'Did he?'

'His wife says so. A car was sent to collect him from
his house one night, the driver was heard to say. "Mr
Hollander wants to see you", and he grabbed his coat and
went with the driver without hesitation.'

'I am not the only Hollander in the Vale.'

'No . . . probably not . . . but it's such an unusual name
that the others will be very easy to trace and eliminate.'
He glanced at the oil painting on the wall, the mahogany
sideboard; he felt the deep-pile carpet beneath his feet.
Hollander had clearly many reasons to stay out of prison,
all the easier to 'rattle his cage', as good old Tam Galloway
would have said. He paused and then said, 'Jane Seymour.'

'Who?'

'You remember her, she accused you of indecent
assault.'

'Oh, yes.' Hollander waived his hand in an imperiously
dismissive gesture.

'No truth in that?'

'None. I think she might have hoped to blackmail me:
accuse me of something, then drop the charges. I never
even knew her.'

'So I believe. I read the file. You signed a statement to
that effect.'

'Yes.'

'But you see our suspicions, Mr Hollander. Your

uncommon name keeps popping up in all the wrong places, it's associated with four murder victims and that boy who was going to give evidence about seeing Jane Seymour at your house . . . he disappeared.'

'Yes,' Hollander said. 'So I believe.'

'Convenient for you.'

'What are you implying?'

'That you had him murdered like you had Gary Sledge murdered, like you had Silcock and Pomfret murdered, like you had Jane Seymour murdered.'

'You'd better be careful what you are saying.'

'Why? Or you'll have me murdered too?' Again Hennessey paused. 'You see the great advantage of visiting by myself and talking to you, and only you, is that I can say what I like. No witnesses. Can be useful, as I am sure you have found out a number of times, which brings us back to young Gary Sledge and the race.'

'The race?'

'The race between you and the police. Gary Sledge had something you wanted, that's why he was tortured. What he had and what you wanted were photographs which showed you and Jane Seymour together. If those photographs come to light then that's your alibi shot. By signing that statement to the effect that you didn't know Jane, you have locked yourself into an alibi. If we can find those photographs, your alibi is blown out of the water and you are in the frame for her murder. So the race is on . . . you will get to them first, the photographs – and the negatives, especially the negatives and you'll continue to live in this opulence –' Hennessey stood – 'or we will . . . or we'll get to them first.'

George Hennessey began to drive home. He had enjoyed the look of colour draining from Hollander's face and had enjoyed watching the confidence evaporate from the man.

It had been a successful visit. Then, on impulse, he allowed his car to slow to a halt at the roadside. He remained stationary with the window down listening to the birdsong and enjoying the vista of the lush, rolling countryside. He then drove on, slowly, not to his home but rather back towards York, to the village of Skelton, north of the city, and within the village to a half-timbered, black and white, detached house. He parked his car at the kerb in front of the house and walked up the driveway, his shoes crunching the gravel as he did so. He was pleased that she had taken his advice and spread the gravel . . . it was, he thought, one of the the best burglar deterrants. He knocked gently on the door, just two taps on the metal knocker and then stepped back from the threshold.

Louise D'Acre opened the door, holding a tea cloth in one hand and, having changed her clothing, was by then dressed, fetchingly he thought, in cut-down jeans, a blue T-shirt, and flip-flop sandals. She smiled at him as she said 'helloooo . . .' warmly extending the 'o' in 'hello'.

'Don't you think that was reckless?' she asked as they sat opposite each other at the stripped pine table in her kitchen, sipping long tonic waters, cooled and refreshed with ice and slivers of lemon. 'He sounds a dangerous man.'

'No, it was safe . . . even calling alone on Hollander was safe. Being a police officer has some protection and I was calling unannounced.'

'Well, that could have gone either way.' She spoke sharply.

'Yes . . . yes I suppose it could, but folk knew where I was and I told Hollander that.'

'George –' she slid her hand across the table top and took hold of his – 'it was still a reckless thing to do. You walked into that house. It's huge by the sound of it . . .'

'It is huge.'

'So you were in danger. You play by the rules. People like Hollander – they make up their own rules. There was plenty of time to do you in and clean up the mess, if any, and get rid of your body. He wouldn't deny you had been in his house – just deny having harmed you or knowing of your whereabouts, or rather the whereabouts of your body . . . Being a police officer wouldn't help you then.'

'Yes . . .' Hennessey nodded. 'I suppose it was a bit . . . risky . . . silly really.'

'I worry about Daniel doing reckless things but you are too long in the tooth to believe you have been blessed with immortality.'

'I am not sure that that is a blessing, if you know what I mean . . . ?'

'Heavens, George, I don't want to see the inside of your body.'

'Strange, isn't it?' Hennessey smiled.

'What is? I am serious about this.'

'So am I. No, what strikes me as strange is that we met over a corpse, our fingers touched for the first time over ice-cold flesh . . .'

'Yes, I asked you to examine a knife wound. Was that the first time we made bodily contact?'

'Yes, it was.' He smiled at her, looking her in the eye. 'I remember it well. How many other couples can say that they met over a dead body . . . and that is something we still have in common. Death employs both of us . . . in a sense.'

'Bizzare.' She laughed, seeing the humour in their situation. 'How much has grown because one man stabbed another with a knife which made a distinctive wound and which caused me to invite you over to take a close look at it.'

After a pause during which both enjoyed an emotional glow of closeness, Hennesey asked, 'For what puposes could a murderer use a deep freeze?'

'Two I can think of instantly. I think I said earlier, it will cause death without leaving any injuries. In which case, it would be difficult to ascertain the cause of death of the body once allowed to thaw . . . fully thaw. That would be difficult to achieve in a corpse, but it could be heated so that the core would thaw. That would be one reason . . . the other reason is to frustrate identifying the body. If the corpse was kept in a deep freeze for a number of years . . . ten, fifteen, twenty years and then left on the road side, it will look fresh and be treated as a recent death. If things were further complicated by the murder being of a man in Kent, whose beautifully preserved body was found, without any identification, in Aberdeenshire, then the Grampian police wouldn't link him with a man who was reported missing in the South of England so many years earlier.' She raised her eyebrows. 'Very useful things deep freezes, if you are a murderer who enjoys playing devious games.'

'I see . . . thanks . . . and Hollander, yes, you are right – it was a silly thing to have done. In fact it might come to haunt me – it's already on my regret pile.'

'Well, you have learned . . . So . . . are you staying the night?

Eight

in which two more arrests are made and further links are unravelled.

Dillet Builders operated from a yard in Fulford. Yellich halted the car outside the premises and he and Hennessey got out and walked up to the gate. The yard, set amid housing, was fenced off with wire, topped with barbed wire. The yellow pickup described by Harvey Longfellow was parked in the yard between a neat pile of breezeblocks and a wooden hut. An Alsatian on a long chain barked aggressively. Yellich lifted the padlock that held the gates together and then let it fall.

'Bit early for them.' Yellich tapped the padlock.

'Ought not to be.' Hennessey glanced at his watch. 'Not if they want to stay in business. I pass a building site on the way in; they were already hard at it by eight thirty.' He took off his hat and wiped his brow. Sweating at this hour, he thought, this one was going to be a hot one. 'We'll wait.'

The two officers waited on Fordland's Road for a further ten minutes, across the road from Dillet's Yard, when a man turned the corner from Fordland's Crescent and shuffled discontentedly, it seemed to Hennessey and Yellich, towards the yard. At the yard gates he stopped, took a key from his pocket and unlocked the gate. The Alsatian barked less aggressively but barked nonetheless. The man walked past the animal, giving the beast no attention. It clearly was not a pet. The man unlocked the door of the shed within the yard and entered it.

'Do you think he could be described as "well-built, frizzy hair, bearded"?' Hennessey turned to Yellich.

'Oh, I think so, boss,' Yellich said. 'Most well built, most frizzy of hair and definitely bearded.'

'Well, let's go and make his acquaintance.' The two officers crossed the road and entered the threshold of the yard, but their further progress was blocked by the snarling and barking Alsatian. The commotion caused the bearded man to step out of the shed.

'Help you?' He spoke with a strong Yorkshire accent. Hennessey thought his manner was more aggressive than businesslike, but in fairness, most of his custom would come by phone, not 'cold calling'; he did not, after all, run a shop.

'Hope so.' Hennessey smiled. 'Police.'

'Oh . . .' The man suddenly looked worried. He glanced round and behind him but the fencing erected to keep thieves out was also keeping him in. 'What's it about?' He raised his voice to carry over the distance between himself and the officers, and to carry in terms of volume over the dog's bark.

'We're not going to compete with the dog, and no point in entertaining the neighbours.'

The man hesitated. Then he went back into the shed and returned a few moments later, carrying a plastic jerry can full of water. He poured the water into a large bowl that stood on the ground close to the point where the dog's chain was attached. The Alsatian stopped barking and went to the bowl and drank deeply. The man returned the jerry can to the shed, closed the shed door and approached the officers. 'Aye?'

'You're Mr Dillet?' Hennessey asked.

'Am I?'

'I was asking.'

'Yeah . . . Robert Dillet. So what?'

'Do you have a partner, business partner, I mean?'

'No.'

'Employee?'

'I take on when I need to.'

'Got someone working for you at the moment? A younger guy . . . clean-shaven, short hair, serious attitude . . . like he never laughs?'

'Might do.'

'Where is he?'

'He'll be in later. There's not much work around at the moment, no point in paying him for eight hours when there isn't eight hours' work to do. Laying someone's drive. We'll pick up the concrete at ten, drive there, have the job done by three this afternoon.'

'And his name is?'

'Prefer you to ask him.'

'Well, we're asking you.'

'Harry Bowman. Anything else, you get from him.'

'Fair enough.' Hennessey glanced over Dillet's shoulder and saw that the Alsatian, having drunk its fill, had found shade and had lain down but was still eyeing Hennessey and Yellich with undivided curiosity and suspicion. 'So, where were you yesterday, about midday . . . possibly late morning . . . let's say about eleven in the forenoon?'

Dillet shrugged but avoided eye contact. 'Can't remember.'

'Can't remember yesterday?'

'I'm a busy man.'

'Just now you complained about not having sufficient work.'

Again, a shrug of the shoulders.

'Do you know the countryside, Robert?' Hennessey asked. 'You don't mind if I call you, Robert?'

'No . . . and no.'

'Well, you see, I'll tell you about the countryside, Robert. It's a fact . . . I've learned it over time because I am not a country dweller, I'm a townie, but it's true that little goes unseen in the country. Even if you don't see anybody, it doesn't mean you're not being watched.'

Robert Dillet shot a worried glance at Hennessey. This time there was definite eye contact.

Hennessey nodded. 'You were seen. I mean, talk about doing things in plain sight.'

'It was a poacher,' Yellich added. 'Now they are good at keeping out of sight and yes, poachers operate during the day as well as at night. Saw you, and Harry Bowman. He was just a few feet away, gave excellent descriptions of you and Bowman and noted the name on the side of your vehicle. That's why we are here so fast.'

'Dare say we could have come last night,' Hennessey added, 'but we had other things to do and we didn't think you'd be going too far.'

Dillett seemed to shrink, his head sagged. 'I have a business to run. Times is hard.'

'Meaning?'

'We didn't kill them.'

'We?'

'Me and Harry.'

'So what did happen?'

'Got a phone call. I owe money see . . . a lot of money. I was told I'd be let off the debt if I did a little job.'

'Go on . . .'

'I was told to pick up the bodies and take them out of York and dump them. If I did that, I'd be let off the debt.'

'So you did?'

'What can I say?'

'Why involve Harry Bowman? What a mate you are. He's looking at four, five years. Minimum. And that's if you are telling us the truth.'

'I am. See, he owed me money, so I offered him the same deal, because I needed help. Debt is horrible. It's like a millstone round your neck. We were both glad to be rid of it in return for half an hour's work. Seemed a good deal at the time, especially for me. I mean, if Harry didn't pay me I wouldn't break his legs, but if I didn't pay up, I wouldn't be working for a long time ... my business would fold ... I'd be finished. I would have done it alone if I could.'

Hennessey placed his hand on Dillet's shoulder. 'Robert Dillet, I am arresting you in connection with the murder of Raymond Pomfret and Ian Silcock. You do not have to say anything but it may harm your defence if you do not mention, when questioned, anything you may later rely on in court. Anything you do say may be given in evidence.'

Dillet said, 'No comment,' and then glanced to his left and said, 'Here comes Harry now. You can ruin his day too.'

'Rather think he ruined his own day,' Hennessey said. He then waited until the indeed humourless-looking Harold Bowman joined the group and then he said, 'I believe you are Harold Bowman?'

'You believe right.' He too spoke with a strong Yorkshire accent. There was an edge of suspicion in his voice.

'I'm DCI Hennessey and you are under arrest.'

'We was seen, Harry,' Dillet explained. 'I had to tell 'em.'

With Bowman and Dillet in separate cells, and knowing that they had twenty-four hours within which to charge or release them, Hennessey and Yellich sat in Hennessey's office, each savouring a mug of steaming tea.

'So –' Hennessey relaxed in his chair – 'how did you get on at Full Sutton with the Burton–Stafford crew?'

'They're frightened, word has gone round the Hall by all accounts about their involvement in Gary Sledge's murder. They are marked men, on borrowed time. They're in their early twenties and are on borrowed time. They'll be good candidates for turning Queen's evidence . . . they'll need witness protection.'

'We'd offer it to them if there was anything they could offer us, but with Pomfret and Silcock now iced . . . literally, seems their value as witnesses is limited. They'll be charged with conspiracy to murder. That'll keep them out of harm's way for about ten years. They'll have to request vulnerable prisoner status if the long arm of the Sledges' Law can reach inside H.M. Prison.'

'Which it will, I think. A favour done inside for a favour done in return outside, it's hardly unknown, boss.'

'It isn't, is it? Any mention of Jane Seymour and Gary Sledge?'

'Not as an item, but Gary did indicate he had something to hold over Hollander, so they told me, but wouldn't give it out under torture before Pomfret shot him. He said, "I've got him over a barrel. I'm not telling you where they are . . ."'

The phone on Hennessey's desk warbled. Hennessey took his time, put his mug of tea on his desktop and picked up the phone in a slow, leisurely manner. 'DCI Hennessey . . . Yes, he's here.' Hennessey looked at Yellich and mouthed 'for you'. 'Yes . . . put her through.' He capped the mouthpiece of the phone and hissed, 'Little Miss Lyall.' He then handed the handset to Yellich.

'Yellich . . . yes, yes it is . . . yes, £5,000 . . . but if you wilfully withhold information . . .' He pulled the handset away from his ear and said, 'She hung up.' He handed the phone back to Hennessey, who replaced it on the telephone rest. 'She wanted to know if the reward was still extant . . .'

'I gathered.'

'Indicated she knew where they were but wouldn't tell us. You heard my advice . . . ?'

'Yes, correctly given I would say. She strikes me as a bit of a game player.'

'More than a bit . . . but anyway, "they" . . . it was apparently more than an indication that we are looking for photographs . . . it was confirmed.' Yellich paused. 'That was the one big thing I got out of the visit yesterday: those lads were told to look for photographs of Jane Seymour and Hollander. I mean, both of them together, thus destroying his alibi about her murder . . . if they can be found. Can't work out the link between Hollander and Gary Sledge.'

'Well, we know that Sledge's father and uncles were once strong-arm boys for Hollander, but I think there's another link. Hollander knew Jane Seymour . . .'

'Yes.'

'Jane Seymour and Heather Lyall were friends.'

'Of course . . . and Heather Lyall and Gary Sledge were involved with each other, so a direct link . . . Hollander, Seymour, Lyall, Sledge . . . and Heather Lyall knows where the photographs are and she's toying with us. Do you think she's in danger?'

'She's in great danger of being charged with obstruction but she's not in danger from Hollander, otherwise *she* would have been abducted and tortured, not Gary Sledge.'

'Aye.' Yellich reclined in his chair. 'makes sense. Did you see Hollander yesterday? What was that expression you used, boss?'

'Rattle his cage? Yes, I think I succeeded. Saw colour drain from his cheeks . . . enjoyed that.'

'Tell me what happened, skipper. Is he as arrogant as I remember him?'

'It was a phone call.' Dillet looked at the tabletop. 'Just a voice on the phone.' There were four men in the room: Hennessey, Yellich, Dillet and a Mr Fogle, duty solicitor for legal aid work. The twin cassettes of the tape recorder spun slowly, the red recording light glowed, the introductions under the terms of the Police and Criminal Evidence Act had been made. Hennessey asked Dillet to explain what had happened, that he and Bowman should dump two frozen bodies in a field in the Vale of York on a hot summer's day. Dillet shrugged and said, 'It was a phone call.'

'From who? Saying what?'

'From . . . I don't know. Saying a cargo is to be collected and disposed of.'

'The cargo being two bodies?'

Dillet nodded.

'Please answer for the purposes of the tape.'

'Yes, but we didn't know that until we got there.'

'Where's there?'

'Lock-up. Little village called High Cotton.'

'That's where Hollander lives.'

'Practically his front yard.' Dillet shrugged again. 'I mean, it's no secret where he lives.'

'Fair enough . . . but, as you say, it's practically his front yard.' Hennessey paused. 'So . . . Hollander isn't a man who lets his hands get dirty?'

'You know him?' Dillet glanced at Hennessey as if in recognition of one who understood.

'By reputation, if nothing else. Seems to like other people to do his dirty work for him.'

'Aye . . . that's Hollander.'

'But it wasn't him that phoned?'

'No . . . and it wasn't from his house either. I heard traffic in the background, so it was a public call box or a mobile phone. Likely to be a mobile these days, they're closing down public call boxes round our way, nobody uses them. Everybody's got a mobile these days. Anyway, gave us the address of a lock-up . . . went there . . . door was closed but the lock had been forced, recently forced, the damage to the lock was new, so who owns or rents that lock-up won't be involved, that would be too obvious.'

'We'll be the judges of that.'

'Aye . . . well . . . we lifted the door . . . up and over hinge . . .'

'Yes.'

'And there they were, two stiffs . . . and I mean frozen.'

'When was this?'

'Yesterday.'

'Time?'

'Daybreak.'

'Early then?'

'That was part of the deal, had to be collected during the hours of darkness. We were a bit late in fact.'

'And what did you have to do?'

'Well, like I said, take them out and dump them somewhere.'

'Didn't take them far. Why did it take you nearly six hours to travel as many miles?'

Again a shrug of the shoulders, it was clearly Dillet's preferred method of communicating. 'Took them back to the yard.'

'To your yard?'

'Aye . . . we didn't know where to take them. The yard seemed to buy us time; the pickup wouldn't look out of place there. Put an extra heavy tarpaulin over them and sat in the hut wondering what to do. Eventually, it was

Harry, he said, "Look, they're melting, let's just get rid of them somewhere . . . so we did."'

'So how did you know it was Hollander who was behind this?'

'Well, the voice told me I'd be let off the one thousand pounds I owed. I only owed that to Hollander. He may just as well have said Mr Hollander will let you off that debt. It wasn't so much the money, it was more being let off having my legs broken if I didn't pay up. There's no point in asking Harry anything. He didn't know what we were doing until he saw the bodies. He was all for running but I said, do this and you can forget that debt you owe me. Like I said, same deal that Hollander offered me.'

Hennessey patted the file on the murder of Jane Seymour. 'This is what is behind all this.'

'I think so.' Yellich nodded in agreement. 'One, two . . . three murders, all connected with the first murder . . . to cover it up and those are the murders we know of. A man like Hollander doesn't get where he is without turning flesh into bones.'

'You think so?'

'I think so.'

'Don't like him, do you, Yellich?'

'Nope. Not a lot. What I don't like about him is that it's never his hand that's on the trigger, never his hands round someone's neck, never his strength that lifts men into deep freezes.'

'Which is what you think happened to Silcock and Pomfret?'

'Had to be.'

'I'm inclined to agree . . . oh . . .' Hennessey put his hand to his forehead.

'Realized something, skipper?' Yellich took the opportunity to glance quickly out of the window of Hennessey's office whilst Hennessey's eyes were downcast. He saw the grey wall, with tourists atop, drenched in sunlight.

'Yes. I should have clicked as soon as I saw their bodies. Shored-up, my grass . . . that man skates on such thin ice at times . . . I fear he's not long for this world, yet he just survives. He's going to come back to me soon but he knows Hollander. Well, he knows of him. Told me that Hollander had a hit man called "Frostbite". I thought it was a guy's nickname, it suggests the kiss of death. It's the sort of name that a hit man would acquire.'

'But now?'

'Now I think it's a deep freeze.'

'Of course. It would make sense.'

'You know this police force, like all police forces, has its list of mis pers and it also has its share of bodies which are found and identified which show no cause of death.'

'Victims of Hollander?'

'Not all . . . but some, I'll be bound. It would be easy to dispose of someone that way, especially during the winter months . . . snow clears . . . not even snow, just a cold snap . . . east wind . . . fella takes his dog for a walk when the weather has warmed, comes across a body . . . ill clad for the time of year, no sign of foul play . . . death by misadventure. But who's to say the body was not already well chilled by the time it was laid in the snow, or in the woodland when the wind-chill factor had pushed the temperature down to below zero and all sensible folk are snug and warm inside?'

'Who indeed?'

'But the underworld . . . they would know. They would do the dirty work, if Hollander is like you say he is.' A chill ran down Hennessey's spine, such a hot day, window open and he felt very cold. Chill factor, indeed, he thought. Chill factor indeed. 'How many victims are we talking about, down the years? Him and his silk shirts and fancy cigarettes. It's not the murder of Jane Seymour that's behind all this.'

'It's Hollander.'

'Yes.'

'Serial killing by proxy. Not new . . . the godfathers in the Mafia have been ordering murders for years but at least they make it look like murder, like Gary Sledge, a gunshot to the head. Hollander has been getting away with it for years because his hit man is a deep freeze.'

'So, why change his MO?' Yellich asked. 'Doesn't make sense . . . if indeed we are right.'

'Only Hollander knows that, and we are right, as with the young man who was going to give evidence in the trial against Hollander for gross indecency against Jane Seymour.' Hennessey leaned back in his chair. 'Let's just hang around here. Jane was with a group of barmaids who accepted an invitation to a party at Hollander's . . .'

'Yes.'

'A party?'

'Yes, boss.'

'Yet here is his statement, stating that he did not know her . . . never met her.'

'Yes.'

'Despite there being a party?' Hennessey raised his eyebrows. 'He silenced more people than the one person who disappeared.'

'He was the only one who disappeared, boss.'

'He was the only person who was going to contradict Hollander. He met "Frostbite" and his body has not been found. The rest had the frighteners put on them. You know, Yellich, this case is only just beginning. If we manage to nail Hollander for something, we'll spend the next few years visiting him in the slammer asking for his co-operation into the investigation of this apparent death by misadventure some years ago, or this still missing person. I can see it. I can really see that happening. I'll probably be well retired before Hollander's legacy is fully unravelled. That'll be your job.'

'Pleasant thought, that.'

'So, let's find out who else was at the party. Do you know the Mail Coach?'

'Confess I don't, boss.'

'Neither do I.' Hennessey reached for the *Yellow Pages.*

'Aye.' The publican pursed his lips. 'I remember Jane. Nice lassie . . . sort of too nice.' He wore black trousers and a red shirt with a black bow tie. He had very smoothly shaved round his face and his hair was closely cut. Hennessey thought he was in his mid-thirties. 'Too nice by half . . .'

'Too nice?' Hennessey glanced around him. Low beams, dark-stained wood, comfortable-looking chairs. The Mail Coach was clearly a 'posh' pub.

'Well, too nice for pub work. People who work behind a bar see life. You know . . . violence, language . . . you need a bit of a hard edge to your character to survive behind the bar. Jane didn't seem to have that and I was reluctant to set her on but I did because I've been wrong before . . . honest-looking boy had his hands in the till as soon as my back was turned. I mean, not literally, because every penny has to be accounted for, but selling his mates expensive lager and ringing it through as inexpensive beer. He only did it when the pub was crowded so it was some time before I twigged. Then there was little Tina, less than five foot tall, but she'd make a Siberian tiger back up. Didn't take crap from anyone. I thought she'd never survive behind a bar but she proved me wrong. So I thought I'd set Jane on and I was wrong again. She was a good worker, didn't get upset about the fights, handled the drunks chatting her up with style and good humour . . . then . . .' he

171

picked up a glass and polished it, 'then she was murdered. Strangled, if I remember. Her body just left lying some-where. That wasn't good. No one deserves to die like that . . . so young as well. You're reopening the case?'

'Sort of,' Hennessey replied. 'Let's just say it's become relevant.'

'Well, I hope you get further this time. Seemed to me the police lost interest with undue haste.'

Yellich remained silent.

'Do you know if she had any connection with Dutchy Hollander?'

'Well, that was in the air when she was murdered, wasn't it? What he did to her . . . allegedly did to her. She was strangled, that young lad disappeared . . . all very iffy. Parties at his house, parties on his yacht . . .'

'His yacht?'

'Gin palace in Hull Marina. Permanently tied up, never takes it out. More like a floating static caravan than a boat. So I hear. Person to talk to is Olivia.'

'Olivia?'

The publican lifted up the bar hatch. 'She's in the kitchen.'

Hennessey and Yellich walked to the kitchen. 'Be opening soon,' the publican called after them. 'I'd appreciate it if you didn't keep her too long.'

'Alright,' Hennessey replied without turning his head, but thought to himself that they'll 'keep her' as long as necessary, opening time or no opening time.

Olivia revealed herself to be of medium height, short of hair and angular of face. She was slicing lemons and looked curiously at Hennessey and Yellich. 'Police?' she asked.

'Yes.' Hennessey spoke softly, attempting to put her at ease. 'Does it show?'

'Frankly, yes. You walk like cops, sort of confidently, and you don't look like Health and Safety people, and cops or Health and Safety or Environmental Health are the only people Mickey would allow behind the bar. Other than staff, of course.'

'Of course.'

'So how can I help you?' She continued to slice the lemons with smooth, precise movements.

'We are making enquiries about Jane Seymour.'

'Oh.' She hunched forward as if she had been dealt a blow to her stomach. 'Jane . . .'

'We gather from your boss that you remember her, Miss . . . ?'

'Mrs . . .' She showed them her left hand. 'Cannon.'

'Mrs Cannon.'

'I was Olivia Fawcett when I knew Jane. We were students, all of us were, the others have moved on with their lives. Well, I've moved on with my life but not geographically speaking. All the others scattered, went where a good degree will take you.'

'I see. So, Jane?'

'Yes . . . murdered. You read of such but never think you'll know someone who is murdered.'

'No. The night of the party . . . ?'

Olivia Cannon raised her eyebrows. 'Which party?'

'The one at Dutchy Hollander's house. The one where he occasioned her indecent assault.'

'I wasn't there.' Said too quickly to be truthful.

'Yes, you were.' Hennessey paused. 'Don't be afraid of Hollander.'

Olivia Cannon turned to Hennessey. 'That's easy for you to say. The boy who was going to give evidence against him, he disappeared. I was a bit wild then. Only two years ago but it seems like a different lifetime. I'm married now; my husband is a university lecturer. We're trying for a family. He's a frightening man and I can't go into witness protection, my husband's job is in York.'

'Anything will help us right now.'

She put the knife down. 'I won't give a statement. If you take me to the police station and conduct a formal interview like on the television, I'll just say "no comment" to every question.'

'Alright.'

'Well, OK, I was at the party. I was at a lot of parties. Jane came that night. She'd been to other parties and to his yacht. Jane had a look of naïvety about her but that was part of her appeal, the unsullied maiden, but she wasn't short of life experience.'

'I get the picture.'

'But she didn't fancy Hollander and drew the line. Hollander thought he got what he wanted, probably still does and wouldn't take "no" . . . that's when the rape happened.'

'It was rape . . . full blown?'

Olivia Cannon shook her head. 'No, it would have been, but she managed to escape, locked herself in a room.'

'Wait . . . she locked herself in? We understood she was locked in by Hollander.'

'Well, what difference does it make? She locked herself in, he said, "Alright, stay there, there's no way out. I'll be out here when you change your mind." So in that situation did it really matter who turned the key? She was still a prisoner . . . well, coerced, I'd say. Either way, non-consensual sex stood between her and her liberty. Anyway, Jane, being Jane, showed she had more about her than Hollander thought and she escaped out of the window, risked her life in the process. Made it back to York and reported the incident to the police, but the only witness disappeared.' She picked up the knife and recommenced slicing lemons. 'Funny that, don't you think?'

'That is something else we wanted to ask . . . a party, yet only one witness. How can that be?'

Olivia Cannon put the knife down again, turned, and resting against the table, folded her arms and said, 'Only one witness was prepared to come forward.'

'What do you mean?'

'Hollander knew he'd gone too far and it wasn't a party . . . not a lot of guests, only him and his minder and four girls and a couple of boys . . . boyfriends of the girls. He knew what he'd done and said . . . I mean, there was an assault before Jane locked herself in the room . . . he'd torn her clothes and taken her shoes, so he said to his minder, "Show them 'Frostbite', Ben."'

'Ben?'

'Yes, that's what he called his minder, "Ben".'

'Not "Big Ben"?'

'No . . . just "Ben" . . . but the guy was hefty. He could well have been called "Big Ben", he could have carried that nickname, easily so.'

'Alright, and then?'

'Well, then things sobered up pretty quickly. We were taken to the cellars of the house and shown a deep freeze . . . opened it. There was nothing in it, it was empty but it was working. Turned up full or down full. Anyway, at its coldest, thick film of ice, and Ben, the minder, said, "If you talk to the cops, you'll disappear but not before you've spent an hour in there . . . and that's all it takes." Then he paused and said, "Don't worry about your friend, as soon as the boss goes to sleep I'll get her away. The dogs are locked up . . . she'll be safe."'

'But Jane got away by herself anyway.'

'Yes, plucky girl. Then she went to the police about the assault. She was strangled and the only boy prepared to give evidence against Hollander disappeared, presumably after he was abducted and reintroduced to "Frostbite". Good way to murder someone, freeze them . . . no sign of injury, even if the body is found . . .'

'That occurred to us.'

'Well that's all I can tell you . . . and that's off the record.'

'Do you know anything about any photographs?'

Olivia Cannon's head sank forward. 'Oh . . . the photographs. Hollander wouldn't let his photograph be taken, but one day . . . on his yacht . . . someone produced a camera, a small one, and started snapping away. He photographed everybody.'

'Was Jane there?'

'Oh yes, Hollander's arm round her. He in a towelling robe and she with only half her bikini on . . . as we all were . . . very hot day.'

'That was at Hull Marina?'

'No . . . that was on one of the rare days that Hollander took his boat out into the estuary. We were away from prying eyes, so the tops came off. The only eyes on us were the coastguards, and then through telescopes, or so we joked. We came back, parked the boat in the Marina and drove back to York. Anyway, Hollander found out about the photos and he was furious . . . tried to recover them, thought he'd got the lot, but Jane had a few . . . about three, she had a notion that they might come in useful.'

'Who took the photographs?'

'A boy called Flynn, Nicholas Flynn . . . worked for Hollander.'

'Where is he now?'

'Don't know, never saw him again . . .' Her voice trailed off as she caught eye contact with Hennessey. 'Oh . . .' her face paled, 'oh . . .'

'Oh, indeed,' Hennessey said.

Hennessey and Yellich returned to Micklegate Bar Police Station. In Hennessey's pigeonhole was a note advising him that a gentleman called 'Shored-up' phoned and would phone back at 2 p.m. Hennessey showed the note to Yellich who said, 'Just time for lunch.'

'Care to join me?'

'No thanks, skipper. I'll go to the canteen. Cheaper.'

Hennessey drove to Doncaster. He parked his car and walked to the railway station. He bought a platform ticket and walked down the steps, through the subway, up the stairs to Platform Three. He walked to the end of the platform. He stood next to Shored-up.

'Flying Scotsman came through bang on time.'

'Really?' Hennessey glanced about him. The bridge over the railway, shunting engines, passenger express trains standing at the platforms, small red and cream multiple units for local passenger traffic moving slowly, people lightly dressed, carrying suitcases, two young women with an immense sun tan, on their way to the Mediterranean after weeks under the sun bed, or on their way back to the typing pool after weeks in the Mediterranean. 'Bit open for you, isn't it, Shored-up?'

'A bit, but if we keep to the end of the platform . . .'

'It's a sight better than Rotherham, I'll say that. I'll never forgive you for insisting we meet there.'

Shored-up grinned. 'But wasn't the information worth visiting the most awful town in all England . . . and Scotland likewise?'

'And Wales too, no doubt . . . but yes, you did well there, can't fault you for that.' Hennessey turned the brim of his hat to the sun.

'Thundered through.'

'What did?'

'The Flying Scotsman . . . at one o'clock, bang on time. Not quite as impressive as the Coronation-class steamers.'

'Are you as old as that?'

'Mr Hennessey, I am what I need to be . . . as young

177

as I need to be . . . as old as I need to be . . . as lofty or as low. It's how I make my living.'

'So I have learned. So, you have information?'

Shored-up pursed his lips. 'Frostbite . . .'

'Is a deep freeze, the type used in hospitals or prisons, big enough to put a body in.'

Shored-up looked crestfallen.

'We worked it out, won't tell you how, but I'll need more than that if you want me to put in a word for you.'

'Yes, I went to see my probation officer. She was not happy with little me.'

'The heavy gates looming, are they?'

The man shrugged.

'Well, you'll need to work extra hard now, won't you?' Hennessey watched a royal-blue GNER train move slowly northwards, picking and snaking her way across the points, under the signal gantry, under the grey road bridge.

'She's off to Edinburgh –' Shored-up followed his gaze – 'calling at York, Darlington, Durham, Newcastle, Berwick-upon-Tweed and Edinburgh . . . passengers for Leeds, Bradford, Leeds/Bradford Airport, Scarborough and Bridlington, change at York. Passengers for Middlesborough, change at Darlington; passengers for Carlisle and Hexham and Sunderland, change at Newcastle; passengers for Glasgow, change at Edinburgh.'

'. . . and passengers for Plymouth are on the wrong train. So what else have I come to the railway crossroads of the north-east for?'

'It is a railway crossroads, Mr Hennessey, on the east-coast main line, lines off to the east and west, and south-east down to Lincolnshire. There are few people whose train hasn't taken them through Doncaster or who haven't changed trains here.'

'Shored-up . . .' But Hennessey guessed he had an ace to play.

'Got a line on Big Ben.'

'And?'

'He's fallen out with Hollander, hasn't he?'

'Has he?'

'So he says ... Hollander, he doesn't like to get his hands dirty.'

'So we have come to understand.'

'Hollander doesn't like spending money, gets the cheapest available or gets people to do his dirty work ... as a means of paying off debts.'

'We've learned that as well.'

'So, cheap workers, or those working to pay off a debt doesn't mean the best. You want quality, you pay for quality.'

'Where's this going?'

'And he replaced people who work for him like you and I change socks.'

'Get to the point before I have the sort of chat with your probation officer that you'd rather I didn't have.'

'Big Ben got turned out. Hollander said he couldn't use him anymore, gave him a grand ... that didn't last long. Replaced him with some youth who will work for half the money.'

'So Ben's angry?'

'Dishing dirt angry.'

'How much dirt?'

'He's prepared to say he saw that girl who was murdered at Hollander's house. He's prepared to say he saw Hollander attack her.'

'That's useful ...' Hennessey's voice trailed off, allowing the female voice to announce the imminent departure of a passenger express to London, calling at Retford, Grantham, Peterborough, Stevenage and London King's Cross. 'But unfortunately, it's not useful enough ... still only his word against Hollander's. We can trace only one other person who saw Jane Seymour at the party and she won't talk. She was introduced to Frostbite, you see, rather had the desired effect. She's still shocked, traumatized by the encounter. One other witness who'll say the same thing and we could discredit his alibi and put him in the frame for conspiracy to murder . . . but as it is, this just hasn't been worth the trip to Donny.'

'I'd like you to meet Big Ben.'

'I think I'd like to meet him. Professionally speaking, of course.'

'Of course.'

'You doubtless could arrange a rendezvous?'

'I'll see what I can do.'

'How soon?'

'Ten minutes. He'll be on his third or fourth pint in the Railway Tavern, but don't worry; he's got hollow legs. The booze has no effect on him, none at all, ex-Merchant Navy, see, and unlike me, he's real.'

Big Ben was very big, carroty hair; huge paws for hands, made the pint glass he held seem nearer to a half-pint in Hennessey's eyes. He had a presence, commanded space, other patrons gave him a lot of space. Shored-up intro-duced Hennessey and, in doing so, Hennessey learned that Big Ben's surname was McLusker. He nodded to Hennessey and said he'd have a pint. Shored-up wanted whisky and ice. Hennessey bought the drinks, had a tonic water for himself and carried the round to the table on a circular tin tray with 'Magnet Ales' written all over it.

'You're after Hollander?' Big Ben spoke with a slow, menacing voice. Hennessey couldn't place his accent. It wasn't northern England, Midlands, he thought . . . Birmingham, Stoke-on-Trent, that sort of area but he couldn't be sure. It wasn't really at all important, anyway.

'Yes.' Hennessey spoke quietly. 'We want him.'

'Shouldn't wonder. You won't get him for all that he's done.'

'That's not unusual. Most people are victims of crime; most felons get away with the majority of their crimes then finally get nailed for one. You can really only serve one life sentence, so one murder will do.'

'You know what I'm talking about then, law man.'

'Yes . . . we know about "Frostbite", the murder of Jane Seymour.'

'And the murder of Gary Sledge?'

'Can't say anything about that.'

'But you are investigating it . . . my ears are close to the ground. So, you are?'

'Yes,' Hennessey said, and intuitively regretted saying it, 'but no proof.'

Big Ben McLusker nodded his head, knowingly, menacingly. Again, despite the stuffy, smoky warmth of the snug in the Railway Tavern, Hennessey once again felt a chill shoot down his spine. What, he thought, what have I just said?

'That's all I needed to hear.' Big Ben McLusker drained his pint and commenced to drink the pint of beer Hennessey had bought for him. He quaffed in deep, manly mouthfuls. When the pint was three-quarter consumed, he asked, 'You got your pen and notepad there?'

'Yes.' Hennessey took his pen and notepad from his jacket pocket.

McLusker turned to Shored-up and said, 'Lose yourself somewhere.' Shored-up stiffened in protest.

'Like Australia,' McLusker growled. 'Somewhere like that.' Shored-up stood, drank his whisky and left the pub.

'Not fair on him.' McLusker leaned forward. 'It's not fair if you know too much, could make things difficult.' He leaned back as the glass collector, collecting empties, took the empty beer glasses from the table and waited while McLusker drained his glass and handed it to her. 'Thank you, pet,' he said warmly as she also wiped the surface of the table.

'Good lass, that,' he said when the glass collector had moved on.

'She is? This your local then?'

'No . . . first time I've been here. I'm on my way south, next train to London.'

'So how do you know she's a good lass?'

'Because she's wiped my prints from this table and she's taken the glasses with my prints on them.'

'You're known to us?'

'Of course, but more than that, I'm wanted. Serious Offence.'

Hennessey felt himself being outmanoeuvred. This man was clearly not to be underestimated.

'My name isn't Ben McLusker. If you type Ben McLusker you'll get a result but the real Ben McLusker is in Long Lartin, doing life for the big M. I just borrowed his name.' The man paused and put his clenched fists into his jacket pocket. "Tiny" Gell . . . write these names down . . . and Andy Cowden. Don't know what "Tiny's" first name is but they're both in Durham, both lifers . . . they murdered Jane Seymour on Hollander's orders. I was there too, but they did the business.'

'Look, I have to caution you.'

'No caution. Just listen. They're ready to cough. And that lad who disappeared . . . any information you want about his death you get from Gell and Cowden but I can tell you where the body is, let his parents give him a proper burial.'

'Where?'

'Near the coast, nearest town would be Hornsea . . . road from Hornsea to Bewholme, on the right as you leave Hornsea, rundown deserted farmhouse, once was a smallholding, grew beetroot. Hollander bought it, didn't want the building, certainly didn't want the business . . . he wanted the land.'

'What for?'

'What do you think, law man? You've got those dogs, the ones that can smell buried bones.' The man stood, hands still in his pockets. 'You release those dogs on that land and you'll get a result. You'll get more than one result . . . that lad and a few others. I dug the holes, some of the holes anyway . . . the whole place is a graveyard.'

'So why are you telling me this?'

'You told me what I wanted to know, so I tell you what you want to know. Gary Sledge . . .' the man shook his head slowly, 'young Gary, he was like a nephew to me.' The man left hurriedly, leaving Hennessey with a sinking feeling in his stomach. He felt for his mobile phone, intending to call three nines but then stopped. It would take ten minutes for the uniformed patrols to arrive, by which time that man would be long gone, and anywhere but the railway station on his way to anywhere but the south. Further, he wasn't going anywhere, that hair, no hiding that, and known to the Sledges and the two felons in Durham Prison. He'd be easy to trace. Hennessey settled back into the chair. It probably hadn't been such a wasted trip after all. He too finished his drink and stood and left the pub. Outside, he discovered that Shored-up hadn't 'lost himself' to Australia or anywhere else.

'He found me, Mr Hennessey.' Shored-up blinked against the sunlight. 'He put the frighteners on me . . . not one of my better favours. He said to give you this.' He handed Hennessey a large wig of red hair. 'I suppose I couldn't ask you for a lift back to York, could I, Mr Hennessey?'

It was, Hennessey later reflected, what going aboard the *Mary Celeste* must have been like.

He had returned, alone, to York and had found Yellich sitting at his desk, writing up a case file. Uninvited, he sat in the chair which stood under the window in Yellich's office. Yellich was the first to speak. 'I think I know where those photographs are.'

Hennessey nodded. 'Among Jane Seymour's possessions in her room in her parents' house at Hutton Cranswick?'

'Yes.' Hennessey rested his hands on his knees. 'We'd better go and collect them if only to protect her parents. I mean, it's only by forcing entry that anybody can get hold of the photographs, and I think Mr and Mrs Seymour have had enough grief.' He paused. 'I met a man a while ago, in Doncaster. He said something which makes me think we ought to bring Hollander in, more for his own safety than anything else.'

'Oh?'

'Yes, my guard was down, I was induced into admitting that we were interested in Hollander in connection with the murder of Gary Sledge ... turns out the guy I was talking to was ... is ... a friend of the Sledge family.'

'Oh ...' Yellich leaned back in his chair. 'Oh ... oh ... oh ...'

'In return, he gave me information about a property out on the coast near Hornsea and two names to be interviewed about Jane's murder. He said Hollander was behind it all ... Jane, and the others in the fields out by Hornsea.'

'Others?'

'I'll tell you in the car.'

The wrought-iron gates at the entrance to Hollander's house were found by Hennessey and Yellich to be open. Not just unlocked, but open. Yellich drove the car up the drive.

'No dogs,' Hennessey remarked.

'Dogs, boss?'

'Yes, he has a pack of Dobermanns and a handler.'

'Gates open, no dogs . . . house looks quiet.'

Yellich halted the car in front of the front door. Dogs were heard barking from beside the house.

'Better check the dogs first,' Hennessey suggested, 'but don't leave the car, for they are many and large.'

Yellich drove the car slowly round the side of the large house and, in doing so, revealed the location of the dogs safely locked up in an outbuilding. A note was securely pinned to the door of the building. Hennessey got out of the car and walked to the door of the building, causing the dogs to bark furiously. The note he saw read 'Dogs have water. Will need feeding today (Tuesday)'. He left the note attached to the door and returned to the car. 'This house has been deserted.'

He picked up the microphone of the car's radio and pressed the 'send' button. Yellich listened whilst Hennessey asked Micklegate Bar to contact the 'animal welfare people' to collect a 'pack of hungry Dobermanns' and gave the address of Hollander's house. Hennessey replaced the microphone and said, 'Let's have a look round.'

The front door of the house was unlocked. Hennessey pushed it open and called, 'Police.' His voice echoed in the building but brought no response. He and Yellich advanced in the building cautiously, yet loudly calling, 'Police. Police. Anyone here? Any person answer.' There was no reply, no response. After twenty minutes going from room to room, the two officers were satisfied that they were alone in the house. There were, however, signs of very recent habitation. A small bedroom at the back of the house gave the impression of having been vacated quickly. Many possessions of female taste had been left behind. Reading the room, it was as if the occupant had been told, 'You've got ten minutes to pack what you can carry'. A second room, which contained more masculine possessions, told the same story.

'You know where we're likely to find Hollander, don't you?' Hennessey turned to Yellich.

'Frostbite.'

Hennessey grimaced. 'I think so. Where would you keep a deep freeze if you had a house like this?'

'Cellar.'

Hours later, when the crime scene had been vacated, Hennessey and Yellich returned to Micklegate Bar Police Station. As they signed in, the duty constable said to Yellich, 'Young lady to see you, sir.' He pointed behind Yellich.

Yellich turned. The young lady was Heather Lyall. She smiled at Yellich but made no attempt to rise from the bench on which she sat.

'It's about the reward,' she said, 'the five thousand pounds. I've decided to tell you where the photographs are.'

'In Jane Seymour's photo album, probably hidden behind other photographs.'

Heather Lyall's draw dropped. 'How . . . ?'

'We worked it out. And nobody's interested anymore, anyway. Had you told us earlier? Well, who knows?'

'So there's no reward?' She paled.

'No. We'll let the Seymours keep their money. It's all they have.'

'But I've booked a holiday . . . paid a deposit . . . non-refundable.'

'Well you'd better unbook it . . . and your deposit . . . well, just look upon that as a fine for withholding evidence. There was a time in this inquiry that we could have used those photographs, but as from about . . .' Yellich shrugged, 'well, about three p.m. today, they became of no use to anybody. We'll let them stay where they are.'

*   *   *

'Prefer calm.' Sara Yellich turned to her husband as she sipped from her glass of chilled Frascati, enjoying his gentle fingertips caressing her arm.

'Sorry?' He allowed himself to be distracted from the late news bulletin.

'Calm . . . "calm" is better than "courteous". Jeremy would find "calm" easier.'

'Yes, it is, and "happy" is better than "honest".'

'It is, isn't it.' I could have done with knowing this technique when I was at school and also later. And "pals" is better than "persons". All Boys Seek Calm Happy Pals. That's much, much better and yes, you're right, Jeremy could cope with that and similar memory aids . . . not yet, but in time.'

SATURDAY, 14.00 HOURS

The middle-aged man and his slender middle-aged lady stood arm in arm against the railings at Whitby Cliff top. They gazed out across the flat North Sea. Blue sky.

'So, that was it, rough justice in the end. We found Hollander in his deep freeze. If that man, who ever he was, had phoned the Sledges the instant he left the Railway Tavern in Doncaster and if the Sledges had got their skates on, they would have been at Hollander's house one hour . . . one and a half hours before Somerled Yellich and I got there.'

'That would have been plenty of time,' the woman replied. 'More than sufficient. If the deep freeze was airtight, he would have suffocated before he froze. I did note broken fingernails . . . he knew what was happening to him. Three minutes without air and you're brain dead . . . another ten minutes and you're lucky dead.'

'Of course, nobody on Tang Hall knew anything about it, nobody would talk to us. The two guys in Durham,

Gell and Cowden, coughed to the murder of Jane Seymour. They'll be going "G" as my son would say, using duress as defence . . . it's a mitigation. It's a good deal for them, their sentence will be swallowed by the sentences they're already serving and they won't have to worry about it once they're released. If they didn't cough to it, we'd have arrested them at the gate in ten year's time.'

'Still seems little to pay for a life of promise taken so young.'

'Yes . . . yes, it does. The information about the old smallholding by Hornsea proved to be solid: five bodies, all identified, one of which was the young man who was prepared to give evidence against Hollander in respect of the attack on Jane Seymour. So his family can bring some closure to that.' Hennessey turned to the lady by his side. 'Well, what do you say? Back to the hotel for the afternoon . . . then dinner . . . then another very early night?'

'Just like last night.' Louise D'Acre smiled and squeezed his arm with hers. 'Yes, I'd like that. I'd like that a lot.'